Also by Rowan Coleman

Ruby Parker: Soap Star
Ruby Parker: Film Star
Ruby Parker: Hollywood Star

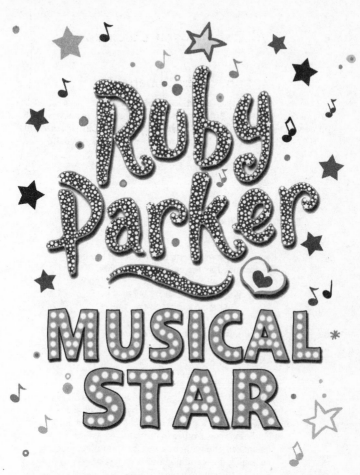

ROWAN COLEMAN

HarperCollins *Children's Books*

For Lily

First published in Great Britain by HarperCollins *Children's Books* 2008
HarperCollins *Children's Books* is a division of HarperCollins*Publishers* Ltd
77-85 Fulham Palace Road, Hammersmith, London W6 8JB

www.harpercollinschildrensbooks.co.uk

1

Copyright © Rowan Coleman 2008

Rowan Coleman asserts the moral right to be
identified as the author of this work.

ISBN-13 978-0-00-724434-8
ISBN-10 0-00-724434-7

Printed and bound in England by
Clays Ltd, St Ives plc

Mixed Sources
Product group from well-managed
forests and other controlled sources
www.fsc.org Cert no. SW-COC-1806
© 1996 Forest Stewardship Council

FSC is a non-profit international organisation established to promote the
responsible management of the world's forests. Products carrying the FSC
label are independently certified to assure consumers that they come
from forests that are managed to meet the social, economic and
ecological needs of present and future generations.

Find out more about HarperCollins and the environment at
www.harpercollins.co.uk/green

SPRING FEVER A GO-GO!

We hardly know where to put ourselves in the *Hiya! Bye-a!* office this week, so excited are we by all the news and gossip that's been landing on our desks.

What could be more thrilling than the dramatic conclusion to *Kensington Heights'* character Marcus Ridley's rollercoaster of a storyline? Actor **Danny Harvey** must surely be hoping to cash in this award season after a spectacular climax involving an explosion, a train crash and a priceless Ming vase. We don't give away secrets here in the *Confidential* column, so you'll just have to watch the show to see what happens – but it's pretty incredible. Is Danny leaving the show for good, we hear you cry? Not according to his people, who assure us the talented youngster is just taking a break to concentrate on his schoolwork and some other projects...

MICK CARUSO

After Danny's hit single, is it possible that one of those projects could be the exciting one-off world premiere performance of a new musical by rock legend **Mick Caruso?**

Mick has been a global household name almost since *before* rock and roll was invented, and we all know and love classic tracks like *Rock Me This Christmas* and *Rock Generation*. Now Mick is putting together a new musical for young people to perform in, in schools and colleges across the land. **Spotlight! The Musical.** revolves around a hopeful young actress at a tough stage school and features some of the greatest hit songs of his career. Excited? We know we are – but wait there's more...

The first ever performance of the musical will take place on primetime television in front of millions of viewers. And that's not all! Televised open auditions for the lead roles and a special schools' choir competition start around the country next week. If you are under sixteen and a star in the making, or you know anyone who is, then you can find out more about the auditions on

hiyabyea.com/spotlight...

HOLLYWOOD HIGH

HUNTER BLAKE

• •

One fledgling star who's taking UK TV by storm is the lead in the hit US imported show *Hollywood High*. **Hunter Blake** is rumoured to be visiting these isles again in the next few weeks to investigate the possibility of making a film about the young Robin Hood, along with Hollywood golden girl **Imogene Grant**. We'll keep you posted on any more details that come to us at *Confidential* because we know that's one movie we want to target!

Chapter One

I'm normal now. Ruby Parker, girl – that's me. Not an audition in sight, not a line to learn or an interview to do, not a single mention in *Hiya! Bye-a!* for weeks. I haven't even had any fan mail for over a month. I used to be Ruby Parker, soap star and then for a while I was Ruby Parker, film star. For the briefest moment I was Ruby Parker, Hollywood star – but now I'm none of those things. I'm just Ruby Parker, who goes to an ordinary school and hangs out with ordinary kids.

It did take a bit of getting used to.

When I got back from Hollywood I think I was in shock. I don't really know what being in shock is, but if it means feeling numb from the inside out, exhausted and frightened all at once, then I was in it. My life had changed completely in the few weeks I was in America and I wasn't really prepared for how it was going to make me feel. But I decided to leave Sylvia Lighthouse's Academy for the Performing Arts and give up acting for good, and I meant it. It took a while to persuade mum and dad to support me, and Nydia and Anne-Marie still can't believe that I decided to come to a new school and leave them behind, but I did it. I gave up my dream because being in Hollywood taught me two things.

First of all it taught me that having a dream isn't enough to make it come true. Wanting fame and fortune so badly that you feel twisted up inside doesn't mean you deserve to get it, because you only deserve your dream if you've got the talent to make it happen. And secondly it told me about as clearly as possible that I do not have any talent. At least, not nearly enough to deserve my dream.

And that's why I started at Highgate Comprehensive School three weeks ago, a school that doesn't even have a drama society, let alone drama lessons. The nearest thing they have to anything theatrical is a choir and I hear even that is terrible. It's a school where I can feel safe, which is funny really because on my very first day I discovered that someone here is really quite keen to beat me up.

It happened in the first minute of the first hour of my first day. I made mum drop me off round the corner, took a breath and marched the last few metres through the school gate on my own. I thought I was prepared.

I was prepared for the other kids to be a bit curious,

to ask me questions about being on the telly and in a movie with famous actors like Imogene Grant or Sean Rivers. I was prepared for the fact that some kids would think I was posh and stuck up because I used to go to Sylvia Lighthouse's Academy. But I wasn't prepared for the threats of violence. Yes, that did throw me a bit.

"Are you Ruby Parker?" asked a tall girl, who appeared to be waiting for me.

This is nice, I thought. *A welcoming committee*. "I am," I said with a smile, sticking out my hand. "Pleased to meet you!"

"I hate you," the girl said. Well, more like growled.

I blinked at her. She had a sort of solid-looking body that would probably hurt you if you ran into it. As I was planning to run in the opposite direction, I hoped that wouldn't be a problem.

"Really?" I asked her, with a grimace. "Was it the film? I know, I was terrible wasn't I? That's why I've given up acting, I just want to be normal now, like…"

The girl's face didn't move. "I just hate you," she said, poking me in the shoulder with the tip of one long finger. "And I'm going to get you." Then she turned on her heel, and stormed off.

I stood there staring after her, suddenly not sure that I could get my feet to go into Highgate Comprehensive School after all and wondering about the possibilities of home-schooling, when I felt a tap on my shoulder.

"That's just Adele." I jumped at the sound of a new voice and a saw another girl standing next to me. "You're Ruby Parker. I've seen you on the telly," she said. I couldn't tell if she was friendly or not. "I'm Dakshima, I'm in your class. Adele tries to pick on everyone, but if you show her you're not scared you'll be fine. She doesn't mean it really. It's just her thing, being scary."

I stood there stock still as Dakshima began to walk off again. After a few steps she paused and glanced back over her shoulder at me. She heaved a sigh and asked, "Do you want to come in with me?"

"If you don't mind," I said, sounding more than a bit pathetic.

"Come on then," Dakshima said, turning and marching off ahead of me. "I haven't got all day."

I followed Dakshima, telling myself that I was doing the right thing, but I still felt sick with nerves and worried about making new friends. After all, I thought I'd made friends with Adrienne Charles at Beaumont High, my school in Hollywood, but she turned out to be my worst enemy and made my life a misery while I was there.

Dakshima doesn't seem to mind me hanging out with her though. I have lunch with her and her friends, Talitha and Hannah, almost every day, and last week she even called me Rubes. It took a while for people to forget that I am Ruby Parker off the telly, but now I'm old news, like last month's copy of *Hiya! Bye-a!*, and the more they forget who I used to be, the easier it is to fit in. Anyway, if you take away the whole fame thing then I really am a very average girl.

The teachers here are very different from the ones at the Academy, but they are mostly OK. I even like the schoolwork. Honestly I do, because when I'm immersed in biology or maths or something that would usually make me tear my hair out with boredom, then I'm not thinking about the past. I'm not thinking about Danny Harvey chucking me for new girl Melody. I'm not thinking about the horrible reviews I got in Hollywood, detailing just how bad an actor I am. And most importantly, I'm not thinking about my dream, or the fact that at almost fourteen-years-old, mine is already so over.

Come and audition for the school choir!

Lunchtime tomorrow in the main hall. Enthusiasm more important than talent. Find out that singing CAN be fun!

Be there or Be square.

Mr G. Petrelli, Music Teacher.

NB: ATTENDANCE IS COMPULSORY BY ORDER OF THE HEAD.

Chapter Two

"So you haven't heard from Hunter once?" Anne-Marie asked me as I screwed up the handout that was in my school bag and dropped it into the paper bin. (I have two bins now, one for paper and one for rubbish I can't recycle. Me and mum are saving the environment; it's our new thing we do together since I ran away from Hollywood and nearly scared her to death.)

I shook my head, "Nope," I said. "Not even a text."

"But after you got back from Hollywood he came all the way to London just to kiss you at the Valentine's disco!" Nydia exclaimed. "I thought he really liked you."

"He didn't come all this way *just* to kiss me," I said, feeling a little blush as I remembered the moment. "He came over to do publicity for *Hollywood High* and he might not have even come to the dance at all if you two hadn't got in touch with him. The whole kissing me thing was sort of an accident. It's not as if it we were meant to be or anything."

To be honest, I was more sad about not hearing from

Hunter again after the Valentine disco than I let on. OK, I told him I didn't want to be his girlfriend, but I had thought he might not take it quite so literally. We had become good friends while I was at Beaumont High and we'd been through a lot together in Hollywood. But I hadn't even had an e-mail from him, even though I'd sent him one when I found out that *The Lost Treasure of King Arthur* was the biggest grossing foreign language film in Japanese history.

"It's just as well anyway," I said casually. "Going out with yet another international teen megastar would not have fitted into my new life at all. I have a lot of homework these days."

"About that," Anne-Marie said, opening my wardrobe and going through my things with her usual wrinkled nose. "Are you still sure about leaving the Academy? Hasn't three weeks with the public been enough to convince you to come back?"

I shook my head and laughed. Anne-Marie called everyone who wasn't an actor/singer/model "the public". She couldn't understand how anybody would be happy just being an anonymous person just living an ordinary life.

"I like my school," I told her. "It turns out I'm quite good at biology and I had a careers talk last week. I think I'm going to be a vet."

"A vet!" Nydia shrieked. "I'm sorry, Ruby, I just can't see it. You faint at the sight of blood."

"Being a vet is not all blood," I said, annoyed that I hadn't spotted the rather obvious flaw in my plan.

"No, there's vomit and pus too, I believe," Anne-Marie said, laughing. "Ruby Parker, vet. Yeah, right."

"This is so wrong," Nydia said quite crossly. "You are meant to act!"

Of my two best friends, Nydia was the one who understood least why I had left school. And I knew why. We started at the academy together when we were little girls and had been together almost every day since. We were like twins, except we're not. We fall out like friends do and fight sometimes, but in the end we have always been there for each other. When my mum and dad split up it was Nydia who helped take my mind off it. And when she fainted and hurt herself because of a stupid diet she was on, it was me who helped her get back to normal and feel better about herself again. When I left, she thought I was leaving her too and, worse, that I was just giving up. An Academy pupil never gives up. It's actually in the rules.

"It's not wrong because I'm happy, Nyds," I told her. "Nothing to worry about, no auditions or interviews. It's great, just like Sean says."

"Except Sean hasn't given up forever ever; he's taking a break while he learns his craft," Anne-Marie reminded me as she held one of my tops up against her. I nodded, even though I wasn't sure that was quite Sean's view of things. Once Hollywood's highest earning child star, Sean had given it all up at the age of fifteen to come and live in England with his long lost mum, go to school at the Academy and be Anne-Marie's boyfriend. He loved acting and singing, but he hated celebrity, especially as his fame and money-mad father had worked him so hard that his life had been miserable. Just before I started at Highgate Comp, he told me he understood exactly why I was doing this.

"I think it's pretty radical," he'd said. "Giving up acting would be like giving up breathing for me, but it if makes you feel better then it's got to be right."

"Can you tell Anne-Marie that?" I'd laughed. "She thinks I'm crazy!"

"She thinks *I'm* crazy." Sean grinned. "So it probably won't make any difference."

I was fairly sure that Sean thought he'd give up fame forever, but Anne-Marie didn't really get that yet.

"The thing is, you've got proper talent," Anne-Marie said, exasperated. "You deserve all the fame and the fortune because you've worked for it. Not like Jade

Caruso – what's she ever done, and she gets her very own musical on TV?"

"What *are* you on about?" I asked. One thing I definitely didn't miss about the Academy was Jade, her catty sneer and her permanently arched eyebrows, always on red alert to make a mean remark.

"Haven't you heard?" Nydia exclaimed. "Jade's dad, Mick Caruso, has written a musical. At least, it's based around all of his hit songs from the last million years or something. He's calling it *Spotlight* and it's set – wait for it – in a stage school."

"He's got together with this writer bloke and they made the songs into a story," Anne-Marie added. "I think it's supposed to be put on in schools and things all over the country, but to launch it he's doing this one-off live TV performance on the BBC for charity."

"Oh," I said, feeling a bit confused. "And?"

"*And*? Almost all the actors in it are to be kids aged between twelve and sixteen. And guess who's auditioning for the lead role?"

"Um…" For one horrible moment I had visions of my Hollywood nemesis Adrienne Charles coming all this way across the Atlantic just to harass me.

"Jade Caruso, you idiot," Anne Marie told me, flinging her arms in the air. "Her daddy couldn't buy her any talent so he gave her a TV musical instead!"

"Jade can't be the lead in a musical," I said. "She's an even worse singer than me!"

"I know," Anne-Marie exclaimed. "And that's saying something."

"Well, to be fair to Jade," Nydia interrupted, making Anne-Marie roll her eyes, "Mr Caruso is holding open auditions and Jade says she has to go through them like everyone else. She's told her dad she doesn't want any special treatment."

"Really?" I asked, looking at Anne-Marie in disbelief.

"You know that you should be at those auditions, don't you?" Anne-Marie asked me. "You and Sean should *both* be there."

When she said that I felt something go off in my tummy, like a spark – a little flicker of how I used to feel about acting. Chances like the one Jade was getting should be earned and not bought, and was she really going to earn it? Then it hit me – who was I to talk? I got offered a film part and a TV role all because at the age of six I was picked at random to be in a soap opera. I hadn't earned any of my chances and as soon as my talent had truly been tested, it had failed miserably.

"But Sean's not going, right?" I asked her.

Anne-Marie sighed and flopped down on my bed.

"No, he's not. But that shouldn't stop you!"

"The last thing I want is to ever go to another audition," I assured her. "I'm with Sean on this one."

"Anyway," Nydia said, looking at me sideways, "even if Jade does get through the open auditions, the final decision is going to be made by a public vote on a live televised final. There's no *way* they can rig that result."

"Oh, you are so naïve," Anne-Marie said, rolling her eyes again. "They do it all the time! She's bound to get the lead."

"Only if you two don't go in for it," I told both of my friends. "I hope you are."

"Course we are," Anne-Mare said. "Sylvia Lighthouse didn't give us a choice, but we would have anyway. The whole school is, apart from Sean. You should see Danny – one rubbish hit record and he thinks he's Justin Timberlake. He's sure he'll get a male lead and I wouldn't be surprised if he does because Jade's still got her eye on him even though he's going with Smelody Melody... oh, sorry."

"Don't be. I don't care," I lied. Mum had told me I'd get over Danny before I knew it, but so far no luck. Not even a lovely kiss with the gorgeous Hunter Blake had worked. I kept my feelings to myself though, because the last thing I needed on top of all the other humiliation I had suffered was to be the girl that Danny Harvey didn't fancy any more.

"And there is no way we can get you to audition?" Nydia asked me. "What if we brought you cakes? Double chocolate cookies?"

I laughed and flopped back on to my bed. "No, I'm not going to audition," I said firmly, feeling surprisingly happy about saying those words out loud. I ticked the reasons off on my fingers. "Number one, because I've given up show business, or hasn't anyone noticed? Number two, because I can't sing. And number three, can you imagine the look on Jade's face if I turned up? Smug-a-rama!"

"She would be hideously smug, that's true," Anne-Marie conceded.

"We'd never hear the end of it," Nydia added sighing. "But Ruby, just think – if you auditioned and went through to the live televised final and *then* got a lead role and *then* was brilliant and *then* all the critics loved you, *then* how smug would Jade be? Hey? Not very, that's how."

"Look, Nyds, thanks for still believing in me and all that – but this is it. This is me now, OK?"

"OK," Nydia said, deflating. "If you say so."

Anne-Marie picked up the DVD she'd brought. "So

when are we going to watch this then?" She asked me, changing the subject.

Just then the doorbell sounded.

"That'll be Dakshima," I told her. "Put the DVD in while I go and get her. And be nice to her, she's the nearest thing I've got to a friend at Highgate and it's a big deal that she's come over tonight. Don't freak her out!"

"Seriously, is that Anne-Marie for real?" Dakshima asked me as I walked out to her dad's car with her a couple of hours later. "Nydia is cool, but the other chick is just weird. She's all plastic fantastic. She's a stage school Barbie."

I tried not to laugh as I glanced up at my bedroom window where Anne-Marie was no doubt being just as rude about Dakshima. The first meeting between my old and new friend hadn't gone as well as I had hoped. Nydia was just Nydia, all lovely and funny. Dakshima made it clear she wasn't impressed that Nydia had been on TV quite a lot, but soon the two of them were hitting it off just like two girls the same age with a lot in common should do. Anne-Marie was completely different. She was like the old Anne-Marie, before Nydia and I had made friends with her – a girl who always seemed aloof, as if the rest of us weren't good enough for her. She barely spoke to Dakshima and when she did it came out either rude or stuck up.

"The thing is," I tried to explain to Dakshima, "she's not really like that. I thought she was a total cow too for ages, and she thought *I* was one, but she's just shy and when she meets people she doesn't know she puts on a front. A lot of us actors... a lot of actors are really shy. I know it seems weird that they can jump about on stage in front of hundreds of people, but that's because they are being someone else, when they have to be themselves it's completely different. Once you've got to know her you'll see. She's a really great friend, plus she could take Adele any day of the week."

Dakshima looked sceptical. "If you say so," she said, opening the door of her dad's car. "Cool DVD though. Do you really know that Hunter kid?"

For about one tenth of second I remembered Hunter kissing me. "Well, I've met him," I said. "Not really the same thing as knowing him."

"Well, tonight was a laugh. We should hang out more after school anyway," Dakshima said.

"Great," I said. "I'd like that."

"So are you ready for the choir audition tomorrow?" Dakshima asked.

"What?" I exclaimed. "Oh, I'm not going to *that*."

"Yeah, you are. Didn't you read the letter? The head's making the whole school audition so we can get a choir together for some competition, I'm not sure what it's for, but it should be a laugh. Everyone has to go and sing for Mr Petrelli tomorrow lunchtime. I want to get into the choir, but don't worry if you don't. All you have to do is sing real bad and then you won't get picked."

"Singing badly isn't a problem," I said heavily.

I really didn't want to go to any kind of audition ever again, not even one I wouldn't get picked for. Because even though I knew I didn't want to be in the choir and that I wasn't good enough to be in it, the thought of not being picked made me feel sick inside. And it was wanting never to feel like that again that made me leave stage school.

But it seemed my old life kept on finding me, even if it was only trying out for the school choir. I'd just have to be as bad as I could possibly be. And I am good at that. It's one of my best things.

Chapter Three

"You knew him, didn't you?" Adele said, thrusting her copy of *Hiya! Bye-a!* under my nose as we queued up outside the hall. "Didn't he chuck you?"

I took the magazine out of her hand and read the part about Danny Harvey and Mick Caruso.

"Yes," I said. "I went out with Danny for a bit and then he dumped me for another girl."

"Why did he chuck you?" Adele demanded.

I was learning that although Adele always talked as if she was about to punch you in the face, that in itself didn't *necessarily* mean that she would. And while she hadn't formally withdrawn her threat to "get me", she hadn't actually got me yet either. I was hoping that Dakshima was right and that she wasn't nearly as scary as she seemed. One thing you couldn't comfortably say to Adele, though, was mind your own business.

"Because he liked the other girl more than me, I suppose," I said with a shrug.

"Prettier than you?" Adele demanded.

I nodded. "Probably."

"Stupid cow," Adele said, and I wasn't sure if she was talking about me or Melody. I read further down the page, about the auditions that Anne-Marie and Nydia had mentioned. For a split second the thought of trying out for the show made me feel excited inside – and then I read the bit about the choir competition. My stomach dropped ten floors into my toes.

"That's mine," Adele said, snatching the magazine back out of my hands.

"Is that what we're doing?" I asked her.

Adele frowned at the magazine and then at me. "What?"

"Is that why we have to sing for Mr Petrelli? So that he can get a choir together to enter this competition?"

"That's right. I told you it was a schools competition," Dakshima said, appearing at my shoulder. "Thanks for saving me a space in the queue, by the way." She winked at the girls she had just pushed in front of, who grumbled but didn't say anything because everyone liked Dakshima.

"I'm not going," I said, picking up my bag.

"Hey, hang on," Dakshima said. "You can't just leave. Mr Petrelli's doing a register for every year group. If you don't sing with us now, he'll only make you go back again and sing on your own. What's your problem, anyway?"

"Nothing, there is no problem, but this is a waste of

time. He won't want me in his choir and I just... I don't want to be involved with this. I've given it up. I left stage school, turned down film roles in Japan and *everything*. I don't want to act any more or sing or do any kind of audition. I want to do biology and show an interest in fractions!"

Dakshima frowned at me and tutted, and I worried that I'd blown our fledgling friendship already.

"It's only singing in the school hall, not *The X Factor*. If you're no good, he'll tap you on the shoulder and you can go, and no one will even care."

"That's my point!" I tried to explain. "I don't want to get tapped on the shoulder any more. That's why I left the Academy, because I couldn't take getting tapped on shoulders *any more*."

"What are you on about?" Dakshima asked me, but before I could answer, the hall doors burst open and Mr Petrelli appeared, armed with a clipboard and a determined look. It was too late to escape.

"Right, Year 9, it's your turn now, and let's hope you've got more to offer than Years 10 and 11. At this rate I'll be entering a choir with only four members and we'll never get our hands on the money."

"Are you religious, sir?" Dakshima said as she walked past him into the hall.

"Why do you ask, Dakshima?

"Because you must be hoping for a miracle!" Dakshima said, making the others giggle.

I didn't laugh because my stomach was in knots and I felt like butterflies had moved into my chest. I felt exactly the same as I had the time I auditioned for Oscar-winning director Art Dubrovnik and *that* day I threw up on my feet. This was only a school choir, a bad school choir at that, and I still felt the same. What I didn't understand was *why*.

As Mr Petrelli called the register, I looked longingly at the door and wished I could escape.

"OK," Mr Petrelli called from the stage. We all stood in haphazard lines in front of him, the boys messing around at the back and the girls chatting. Some things never change no matter what type of school you go to. "CAN I HAVE SOME QUIET, PLEASE?" he yelled.

The talking lowered to a murmur and Mr Petrelli switched on an overhead projector. A set of words flashed up on the screen at a slight angle. I recognised them.

"This is how it's going to work," said Mr Petrelli. "If I tap you on the shoulder, you have to go. If I don't, you stay – and don't sneak off because I *will* hunt you down and I *will* make you sing." There was a collective groan. "Now, I thought I'd give you all a song you know so I've picked last year's dreadful Christmas number one, *You Take Me To (Kensington Heights)*."

"Don't make us sing that rubbish," one of the boys called out.

"That's Ruby Parker's boyfriend's song," Adele told everyone at the top of her voice. "Except he chucked her!"

For a second, the whole of Year 9 looked at me. I dropped my chin on to my chest and prayed for a hole to appear in the floor, but God obviously wasn't listening.

"Well then, Ruby, I expect you to be the best," Mr Petrelli said. He pressed play on his CD player and the opening bars to Danny's number one song filled the hall.

"Two, three, four!" Mr Petrelli yelled, waving a baton at us like somehow it was going to make us sing better.

"Before I met you, I was on a dark and dusty shelf.
Oh and I hated myself
Cos I was all alone..."

The whole of Year 9 sang more or less in unison.

"I can't believe I actually have to do this," I complained to Dakshima over the singing, as Mr Petrelli walked long the row in front of us, tapping shoulders as he went. "I thought I had been humiliated about as much as possible for a girl of my age – but apparently not."

"Oh, chill," Dakshima said. "It's only a bit of singing, Ruby, not the end of the world."

It was clear if I was going to be friends with Dakshima then I was going to have to tone down the drama queen thing. But that was one of the things I liked best about her. She made me be *me*, and not some acted out version of the me I thought I should be to impress other people. Dakshima winked at me and just as Mr Petrelli started to walk down our row and I joined in with the singing. After all, I decided, I might as well get it over with as quickly as I could.

"And now, your love lifts me,
So high and so easily.
And I know I'll love you
With all of my might,
Because you
Take me to –
Kensington Heights!"

As I sang I watched Mr Petrelli approaching, tapping shoulder after shoulder as he went. Only two other people from our row were still standing by the time he got to me and Dakshima, and Adele wasn't one of them.

"This is a fix," she said angrily as she marched off.

It seemed like Mr Petrelli stood there for ages, torturing me as he listened to me trying to sing my ex-boyfriend's number one single, and it felt like he was never going to tap me on the shoulder. When he nodded and moved on to Dakshima I realised why.

I, me – Ruby who can't really sing, had somehow made it into the choir without even trying. It was a nightmare!

I stared at Dakshima as he nodded at her too and moved on.

She grinned at me still, singing along to the tune, but inserting her own words now.

"This is going to be so cool," she sang. *"We'll get totally loads of time off of school rehearsing for the competition."*

"I don't want to be in the choir," I sang back. *"This wasn't supposed to happen."*

"Don't sweat it, Ruby," Dakshima replied tunefully, making me realise that she actually did have a very nice voice. *"There's no way Highgate Comp will ever get past the first round!"*

As she finished on the last note of the song with a flourish, I looked around at the few people from our year group that remained. I couldn't believe I was one of them.

"Right, children," Mr Petrelli said, pushing the stop button on his CD player. "Thank you for joining the choir. Rehearsals are every lunchtime and after school starting tomorrow. You can bring a sandwich with you, OK? Now get to class."

"Oh *what*?" Dakshima groaned. "What about all the time off, sir?

"This isn't a game to get you out of your school work, Dakshima," Mr Petrelli told her seriously. "This school is desperate for a new music and drama lab, and winning that prize money is the only way we can ever afford it."

"Excuse me, sir," I said stopping in front of him. "Thank you for picking me to be in the choir, but I don't think you could have really heard my voice. I'm not a singer, sir."

Mr Petrelli looked at me with round black eyes that made me feel a little bit like running away. "If I didn't tap you on the shoulder, then you are a singer," he said. "I am never wrong."

"But at the Academy," I pressed on. "That's Sylvia Lighthouse's Academy for the Performing Arts, I didn't do *any* singing. I did acting, that was all, and I wasn't even very good at that as it happens."

"Look, Ruby," Mr Petrelli sounded impatient. "Perhaps your last school was filled with budding tenors and sopranos, although not if that dreadful single your friend produced is anything to go by. But in this school your voice is in the top ten per cent. Yes, it needs some work, your tuning is off and you sing like a mouse – but you are the best of a bad lot and you are in the choir."

"The thing is," I tried to explain, "I've given up show business, so thanks for the offer but..."

"Ruby," Mr Petrelli said firmly, "I'm not asking you. I'm telling you. At this school a lot of kids would do anything to have a tenth of what you've just thrown away. And as preposterous as it seems right now, this choir is the nearest thing we've got to making that happen. As long as you can carry a tune, you are in it. Understood?"

"Understood, sir," I said, in a small voice. For a music teacher Mr Petrelli could be quite scary, although no where near Sylvia Lighthouse levels.

"Good. Get along to class then," Mr Petrelli told me. "You'll be late for biology."

Adele was waiting for me when I came out of the hall. The corridors were empty except for her. She was standing there, her arms crossed, her brow pulled together in the middle.

"Hi," I said hesitantly.

"*You* got picked for the choir," she said accusingly.

"Yes…"

"I didn't get picked," she growled. I bit my lip. At the very least, Adele and I were now going to be several minutes late for biology and I would be getting detained after school. On the bright side, I wouldn't be able to do detention because Adele would have broken my legs for getting in the school choir I didn't want to be in and I would be in A&E.

Funny, I thought to myself, *life as a normal kid isn't nearly as uncomplicated as I hoped.*

"I wanted to be in the choir." Adele took two or three menacing steps towards me. I found myself thinking about the letters girls used to write to me when I was in *Kensington Heights*, telling me about being bullied at school and how awful it was and how every single night they went to bed feeling sick with dread and would find whatever reason they could not to go to school. But although Adele had threatened to get me on my very first day, I hadn't been nearly as scared of her as I was of Adrienne Charles at Beaumont High in Hollywood. Until now, that is.

"Look," I said, holding up my hands, "I don't want to be in the choir, Adele. I'll get out of it… I'll fake a sore throat or something – I'm quite good at acting, so I think I can pull it off. Then maybe you'll get my place."

"I won't," Adele said, her face get redder and redder. "I never get anything. Always last to be picked in netball, I never have a lab partner in biology and now this. I... I'm... gonna..."

I squeezed my bag tightly to my chest and closed my eyes, certain that I was about to find out exactly how much it hurt to be punched.

After a second or two minus any pain, I realised that instead of hitting me, Adele was making a snuffly, gurgling sort of noise. I opened one eye and, unable to believe what I was seeing, I opened the other just to double-check.

Adele was *crying*.

"Er..." I had no idea how to deal with this. It was like seeing my mum with artificially inflated fish lips in Hollywood – so bizarre I couldn't quite believe it was real. "Oh dear. Um... don't cry, Adele, it's not that bad. I mean, if I'm in the choir then we don't stand a chance of winning anyway, so you're not really missing out on anything. Dakshima says we won't get past the first round."

"It's not that," Adele said, wiping her sleeve under her nose and sniffing.

"Isn't it?" I asked her.

"I'm never included in anything," Adele said. "And I actually can sing pretty well – not like those people on

The X Factor who think they can sing but can't. I'm in the choir at church. But when I got in the hall with everybody there I couldn't do it. I thought if everybody saw me trying they'd think I was even more stupid than they already do and I got all scared and my voice came out all squeaky and off key."

"You know what a key is?" I asked her, taking a step closer to her. "Cos I don't."

"Yes," Adele said. "But no one at at school knows anything about me really, not even the teachers."

"Adele, you should ask Mr Petrelli for another audition, just you on your own. Then you wouldn't have to be so nervous. Trust me, I know what that's like. Once I threw up on my shoes during an audition."

"Serious?" Adele asked me. "That's rank."

"I know! Look, if you wanted... maybe I could help you? At the Academy we used to do breathing techniques and stuff for when you're nervous."

"*You'd* help *me*?" Adele asked me. "You, the famous rich kid?"

"I'm not a..." I paused. The fact of the matter was that I *had* been on TV for years and years, and in one film that a lot of people went to see, even though it was voted one of the top three worst films of the year. And even though I didn't see a penny of it, apart from my pocket money, the chances were that I did have quite a lot of money in the bank. Compared to a lot of other Highgate comp kids, I *was* rich.

"Look, I've been famous, but I was rubbish at it. And I don't want to be famous any more. People say things about you and they don't care how it might make you feel. They think they know what you are like without really knowing you at all."

"Sounds a lot like school," Adele said.

"Maybe it is," I said thoughtfully. "Look, maybe, what with you threatening to get me and everything, I did judge you a little bit. But if you are saying that you are *not*, after all, a homicidal maniac, then I would be very glad to help you."

"I wouldn't have actually ever *got* you," Adele said. "I don't even know why I said it. I was coming over to say hello, but then I thought there's no way that famous rich kid is ever going to be friends with me and before I knew it I was saying what I said. That's how everyone expects me to be."

I smiled tentatively at her and she returned my smile.

"We should get to class," I said. "We're definitely going to get killed by Mrs Moreton."

"No we won't," Adele said. "I'll say I had to take you to the loos because you felt sick, but you're better now."

"OK," I said, looking at Adele's tear streaked face. "Or we could say you were sick and I was helping you?"

"That would never work," Adele said, putting her arm heavily around me in preparation for our roles. "No one would ever believe it."

Dear Ruby

You are invited to Anne-Marie's
fourteenth birthday party!
When? March 15th
Where? Chance Heights, Highgate, London
Wear? Anything fabulous.
Bring? Presents!

RSVP Anne-Marie

Chapter Four

"So who's coming?" I asked Anne-Marie. Her invitation had arrived in the post just before I was due to leave for school, even though I was going to see her that evening.

"Well, of course I posted the invitations," she'd explained when I'd phoned her on her mobile to ask her why she hadn't just given it to me. "It's so much more glamorous – I didn't want to hand then out at school like some little kid. This is the dress rehearsal for my sweet sixteen – it's got to be perfect!"

"But you've got another birthday to go before then," I'd reminded her as I headed for the corner where I was going to meet Dakshima. Today was our first choir rehearsal, one of a handful before the regional finals due to be held in only a few days. It didn't exactly leave Mr Petrelli much time to hone us into a "well oiled singing machine" as he put it, but he was determined to give it a go.

I hadn't told Anne-Marie and Nydia about the choir yet. I don't know why. I suppose that compared to what they were doing, auditioning for the lead roles while I was toiling away in the back row of a third-rate choir, it seemed a bit... well, I'm ashamed to admit, I was embarrassed by it.

"I *know* I've got another birthday to go before then," Anne-Marie said in my ear, probably while putting her lip gloss on because she sounded as if she was trying to talk without moving her mouth. "But this is the *dress rehearsal* for the dress rehearsal. Plus this is the first time Daddy has ever let me have a proper party with a DJ and everything. He said as he's working in LA on my birthday and Mummy will be in Thailand, I could have what ever I wanted, I just had to tell Pilar. I want it to be the best party the Academy has ever seen. Jade might have a rock star father who'll stage a musical for her to be in, but mine says I can have a Chinese buffet and *that's* real class."

"I've always thought so," I said. "So who's coming then? You make it sound like you're inviting the whole school."

"I *am* inviting the whole school," Anne-Marie said. "Oh, and you, of course. I keep forgetting you've left. I still think you should come back here, me and Nydia both do. We miss you."

"You're even inviting Jade and Menakshi and that

lot?" I asked her, ignoring the last bit.

"Yes, I'm *especially* inviting Jade and Menakshi and that lot," Anne-Marie told me. "This isn't about friendship, Ruby, this is about getting as many people as I can to my party. Jade and Menakshi and that lot will come because everybody else is, and everybody else will come because they are. It's very complicated."

"Sounds it," I said, waving at Dakshima as I saw her turn the corner. She nodded at me and then waited, looking in the other direction as if she was keen to be going. "Can I bring Dakshima?" I asked.

"Do you have to?" Anne-Marie sighed heavily. "Only I wasn't really planning on inviting the public."

"Annie," I said, using the nickname that normally only Sean Rivers was allowed to. "Dakshima is the coolest and most popular girl in my year and I want to be friends with her. Inviting her to your party will be a really big step in the right direction. Besides, you might go to a stage school and you might have modelled a bit for H&M, but you are still the public. You haven't won one of the leads in *Spotlight* yet, you know, so don't be such a snob."

"But I am going to get this part," Anne-Marie said. "I just know that I am – this is my year, Ruby. I can feel it!"

"OK," I said. "But don't the *public* vote for the ultimate winners?"

"Yes," Anne-Marie said impatiently, as if the fact was incidental.

"So..." I grinned at Dakshima as I fell into step with her. "Don't you think you should start being nice to them?"

"Oh," Anne-Marie said. "Well, yes, you have a point. OK you can bring Dakshima, but tell her she has to wear a dress and she's not allowed to be rude to anyone."

"OK then." I said, grinning. "I will tell her exactly that. See you later."

"Ciao, Baby!" Anne-Marie said, and was gone.

"So?" Dakshima asked me.

"So," I replied. "Want to go to a party?"

Dakshima, Adele and I stood outside the music room a good ten minutes before rehearsals were due to start. Mr Petrelli had given everyone a chance to get some food from the canteen, but we didn't go. Now was Adele's chance to sing for Mr Petrelli again. I'd told Dakshima all about how Adele wanted another chance to be in the choir and after laughing in my face because she simply didn't believe me, Dakshima decided she wanted to come along and see if it was really true.

"You didn't say she was coming," Adele growled at me as Dakshima and I approached.

"She's come to support you too," I said, peering in through the glass door, where Mr Petrelli was scowling at some sheet music. "Now, remember what I told you?"

We had secretly being doing breathing exercises at her house after school for three nights in a row. It was funny, Adele's family weren't at all like I expected them to be (frightening) and when she was at home she was almost a completely different person. She laughed and didn't look so angry all the time. I couldn't get her to sing for me even though her granny said she had a voice like an angel. Every time I asked her to sing, Adele would blush and tell me she was saving herself for today. It did make me slightly worried that it meant she *was* like those people on *The X Factor* after all – the ones whose mums or grannies said they could sing, but then it turned out they'd been lying and a dead cat could carry a tune better. I didn't say anything about my fears though. I liked smiling Adele; she was much more preferable to scary Adele.

"I remember the exercises," Adele said, putting her hands flat on her tummy and breathing in and out deeply.

"Go on then," I said, glancing at my watch. "The others will be here really soon. It's now or never."

Adele stared at the door handle that led into the music room as if it might be red hot. "Never," she said flatly, turning on her heel.

"Told you," Dakshima said, leaning against the doorframe with her arms crossed. "Like *she* can sing."

"She can!" I said. "Probably." I reached out and grabbed Adele's arm quite firmly. Dakshima's jaw dropped.

"Adele," I said, keeping my voice steady and calm. "Just go in and give it a go. You know how much you want to be in the choir, but you'll never be in it if you don't try." I glanced at Dakshima. "We'll come in with you if you like."

Adele scowled at Dakshima. "You can," she said, nodding at me. "Not her."

"Fine by me," Dakshima said, raising a brow.

"Let's go then," I said, still holding her arm. "Now – before you change your mind again."

Mr Petrelli glanced up at us as we entered. "You're early, Ruby," he said, looking back down at the sheet music. "While I commend your eagerness, I'd prefer it if you waited outside until I call you in." He squinted at Adele over the top of his glasses. "And why are you here, Adele?"

"Whatever," Adel mumbled. "I'm going."

"The thing is," I said, putting my hand on Adele's shoulder, "Adele would really, really like to be in the choir. She didn't do very well in the hall because she was nervous, but she sings in a gospel choir every Sunday so she can't be that bad. We wondered, would you give her another chance, Mr Petrelli, please? Just let her sing a little bit, before the others get here. After all, we need all the singers we can get, right?"

Mr Petrelli looked at me. "This won't get you off the hook, Ruby," he told me. "Even if she turns out to be the next Charlotte Church, you still have to be in the choir."

"I know," I said. "I've come to terms with it, but please give Adele a chance. We've practised breathing and everything." I thought Mr Petrelli almost smiled, but before his twitching mouth could turn upwards, he turned all stern again.

"Well then," he stood up straight, as if bracing himself. "Go ahead, Adele. Let's hear it."

I let go of Adele's arm and stood back, glancing at Dakshima's face peering in through the window of the door. "Remember to breathe," I whispered.

Adele opened her mouth and began to sing *Amazing Grace*, and I watched as Mr Petrelli's expression changed from stern to pure delight. Adele really could sing, and about a million times better than anyone ever on *X Factor*.

"Adele Adebayor," Mr Petrelli said, smiling for the first time since I'd known him. "You have been hiding you light under a bushel."

"A what under a what?" I asked happily.

"It's from the bible," Adele told me. "It means I've been keeping my singing a secret."

"You totally have," I told her. "You totally have been really hiding it under a bushel thingy." I looked at Mr Petrelli. "Well?" I asked him. "Is Adele in?"

Mr Petrelli smiled at me. "Adele is in," he said. "And you know what else?" Adele and I shook our heads. "When I discover a voice like Adele's right under my nose, it makes me realise something rather amazing."

"What, sir?" Dakshima asked, pushing open the door.

"It turns out, Dakshima, that miracles do happen after all."

"Spotlight!"
Words and Music by *Mick Caruso*

First all there is darkness, a silent empty space.
And suddenly you feel it touching your face!
It feels so very good, as warm as the sun,
And when you're in it you know you've become

A star.

Spotlight, spotlight
Come and find me.
Spotlight, spotlight
You can't blind me.
If anyone was ever meant to be
bathed in your golden light - it's me!
If anyone was ever meant to be.

This is where my dreams are, captured in the light.
This is where they come true, right here tonight.
In the golden spotlight I am at home.
No need to run the race any more, because
I've already won it.

Spotlight, spotlight
Come and find me.
Spotlight, spotlight
You can't blind me.
If anyone was ever meant to be
bathed in your golden light - it's me!
If anyone was ever meant to be.

Listen to that applause, it is all for me.

```
I'm standing in the spotlight, being all that I can be.
This is the beginning, a beginning without end,
When you've got the spotlight, you don't need
another friend
So...

Spotlight, spotlight
Come and find me.
Spotlight, spotlight
You can't blind me.
If anyone was ever meant to be
bathed in your golden light - it's me!
If anyone was ever meant to be.
```

"Right now, this time let's try it with some feeling,"
Mr Petrelli said. "Come on, people, we've only got twenty
minutes left. This is it our chance to be in the spotlight –
excuse the pun." The choir groaned as one.

"This," Mr Petrelli went on, "is the central song of the
musical, this is what – if you win a place in the chorus –
you'll be singing on TV in front of millions of people and
you can't tell me you don't like the sound of that!"

The choir blinked at him, somehow Mr Petrelli wasn't
quite selling the being on TV bit to them... *us*, I mean.

Only I'd been live on TV in front of millions and millions of people before and it never seemed to work out so well. Last time had been on the *Carl Vine Show* in America, when I'd accidentally blown Sean's UK location to the world's media, lumbering him with a paparazzi army on his doorstep the very next morning.

"Look," Mr Petrelli tried again. "You've picked up the tune pretty quickly, and amazingly the harmonies actually don't sound *too* awful. But what I need from you, from all of you, is *oomph*. Some razzle dazzle, some..." Mr Petrelli trailed off as he looked at all of us, the best singers Highgate Comp had to offer, staring blankly at him.

When I first met Mr Petrelli I'd thought he was a bit like Sylvia Lighthouse, passionate about his subject and a bit scary. But if he were anything like Ms Lighthouse then he could have frightened us all into performing. But once you got to know him you could tell that he just loved music and singing, and he couldn't understand why everyone else didn't feel the same way. It didn't help that only two of the choir really wanted to be here. One of them was Dakshima, the other was Adele and even she still didn't seem to be able to let herself sing as wonderfully again, a fact that Mr Petrelli was tactfully ignoring.

"We've got one shot at this, people," Mr Petrelli told us. "One shot to get through the regional finals and get our chance to be on TV and win that prize. And maybe we aren't the best choir, but I've heard all of you sing, and whether you believe me or not I know that you all have good voices. Some of them, when I get a chance to work with you, might be truly great. So, come on! I know you can do it!"

If there had been any tumbleweed in the music room it would have blown across the room just then. I think Mr Petrelli was hoping for some whoops, maybe a couple of excited jumps, but all he got back from his pep talk was silence.

"Plus," I piped up from the third row, "if we win, we're bound to meet a ton of celebrities."

"Celebrities?" Gabe Martinez asked me. "Any footballers?"

"Yes, totally," I said, twisting to look at him. "There are always a couple of WAGS and a footballer or two in any celebrity audience. They love the whole TV charity performance thing."

"When I try and think of millions of people seeing us on TV, it doesn't feel real," Talitha Penny said thoughtfully. Talitha was in the year above me and one of Dakshima's best friends. Her younger sister Hannah was in our year and also in the choir – obviously a talent for singing ran in her family. "I suppose it would be cool though. We'd be famous!"

"Yeah," I said, trying to sound all casual. "Completely."

"You've been on telly loads of times, Ruby," Dakshima said. "I remember seeing you and that Sean Rivers at the soap awards last year. Before he went mental. You tripped up and fell flat on your face, didn't you?"

"Yeah, I did," I said, feeling my cheeks colour. I had been trying to chase Danny in a pair of shoes that were far too high for me, because I wanted to tell him that there was no truth in the rumour that Sean and I were dating. What a waste of time that had been. I embarrassed myself on national TV for nothing because Danny chucked me anyway while I was in Hollywood. "Live TV can be... unpredictable. It's different from filming or taping because you know you've only got one shot to get it right... or get it wrong and fall flat on your face." Everyone laughed and I smiled too because it was friendly laughter. "There are millions of people watching you so it does feel pretty weird, but in a good way – you know – exciting."

"I'd like to be, like, famous," Talitha said after a moment.

"And telly famous too," Gabe said. "That's properly famous that is."

"Well, that's good, I think," Mr Petrelli said slowly. "That's a reason to stop messing around and start giving it your all. Because if you people want to stand even the smallest chance of making it on TV as part of the chorus for *Spotlight!* you have to mean every single word you sing. You have to *act* it, *feel* it, *be* it, *love* it. God knows they are awful lyrics, but they're what we've got to work with."

"We've got her, Ruby Parker," Hannah said, pointing at me. "She's been in films. The judges will love that." A few other people murmured in agreement.

"No, I mean, *yes*," I said, flustered. "I mean, you have got me, but this isn't about me, it's about the school and all of us. In fact I'd really rather we played down what I used to do as much as possible because a chorus is like a team. We all have to work together. There can't be any individual that stands out. We're the glue that holds everything else together. If we do that, then we might, just might, be in with a shot of winning."

"And there is one other thing," Mr Petrelli added. "I wasn't going to tell you this, but as it seems fame and celebrity are what motivate you the most, I can tell you that Danny Harvey is going to be auditioning for the lead at the same time you are taking part in the competition. You might even be able to get some autographs."

"Cool," Hannah said.

"He's the one that chucked Ruby," Adele reminded everyone.

"Oh, right," Hannah said, looking at me. "Never really liked him myself."

My heart was sinking, but not because of Danny. If the choir competition and the auditions for the leads were going to be on the same day, I'd have to tell Nydia and Anne-Marie about joining the choir because I was bound to see them, not to mention Jade, Menakshi and the rest. And although I knew Anne-Marie and Nydia would be fine about it, even pleased for me, Jade and Menakshi would find the whole thing hilarious. Failed star, Ruby Parker, tagging along with some manky school choir when she told everyone she didn't want to do anything to do with show business any more. They'd think I'd given up – not because I chose to, but because I wasn't good enough.

And the worst thing, the deepest darkest worst thing was, that I *had* given up because I wasn't good enough. But I didn't want them or anyone else to know that.

I glanced around at the choir and decided to take my own advice. I couldn't get out of this so now I was part of the team, part of what might one day be a chorus. I would do the only thing I could do, blend myself into the background and do my best to help make the choir as good as it could be.

"Right," Mr Petrelli said, gesturing for silence. "Now we've got our motivation – let's sing!"

Chapter Five

It took some persuading to get Dakshima to come to Anne-Marie's party.

"I'm not sure this is really me," Dakshima was still saying while we getting ready round at mine. "I mean, trainers and jeans are me, and hanging out at the multiplex on a Friday night is me. Not wearing a sparkly dress and hanging out with the people who star in the films that are on at the multiplex. That's not me at all."

"There won't be any film stars there," I said. "Only Sean Rivers, and he's retired. In fact, it's probably best to act as if you have no idea who he is, especially in front of Anne-Marie. She can be a bit territorial."

"*Only* Sean Rivers," Dakshima laughed. "You can't say the words *only* and Sean Rivers in the same sentence! I love his film *The Underdogs*. I've seen it about a hundred times. I can't believe he's Anne-Marie's boyfriend. I was sure he'd like normal girls like me."

"Anne-Marie is normal," I defended my old friend to my new one. "Yes, she is *very* rich; yes her dad *is* a movie producer and her mum is a fashion industry mogul. But it doesn't stop her from being one of the best and most loyal friends I have. And it's not all easy for her, you know. She never sees her parents; she spends most of her time alone with the housekeeper and her older brother. Money can't make you happy."

"No, but it can make being sad a lot easier to deal with," Dakshima observed.

"Starting a new school is hard," I tried to explain. "Knowing you, Hannah and Talitha and the others makes it better... easier. I want my new friends to get on with my old ones, starting with you."

Dakshima watched me for a moment as if she was deciding whether we were friends or not. "All right then," she smiled after a moment. "I'll give a go, seeing as you are a movie star too."

"I was in a film," I protested, still feeling a bit awkward about my famous past. "That's a whole different thing."

"Just for the record, I thought that *The Lost Treasure of King Arthur* was pretty good actually," Dakshima said. "Not the best film I've ever seen, like. But I didn't hate it. You were all right in it. And Sean was well amazing... Anyway I've always wanted to go to a show biz party."

"Only an hour till the party – better decide what to wear," I said, opening my wardrobe doors.

I took one of the outfits I had brought home from Hollywood out of my wardrobe; a dark, ruby red velvet dress with a drop waist and a silk rose on the hip. It was exactly the sort of "fabulous" thing I should be wearing to Anne-Marie's party, but I wasn't sure if I could bring myself to do it.

"That's nice," Dakshima said, wrinkling her nose a little bit. "It's a bit girly, but I suppose that's dresses for you."

"It reminds me of Hollywood," I said, thoughtfully.

"Well it's perfect then, isn't it? That's what Anne-Marie wants. For everyone to dress up like Hollywood Stars?"

"I hated Hollywood," I said. "What with getting hounded out of school by the nastiest girl I've ever met, and then hounded out of Hollywood by critics and the press. In the end I ran away, stole my mum's credit card, booked myself a flight and came home in the middle of the night alone because I didn't think mum would let me."

"Weren't you scared?" Dakshima asked me, her eyes widening.

"Seriously scared. I just had to get out of Hollywood, right then. Mum said anything could have happened to me." I paused, remembering how much Mum had cried and shouted at me when she caught up with me. "Anyway, reminding myself about Hollywood isn't the most fun thing, which is why I don't really want to wear this dress."

"Rubbish," Dakshima said firmly, without a shred of sympathy. I looked at her. "That's plain rubbish, Ruby. Put the dress on – you'll look really great in it. And you can't tell me any remotely sane thirteen-year-old girl is not going to wear something totally cool because it reminds her of a place that wasn't so cool. If you wear that dress tonight then from tomorrow it will remind you of Anne-Marie's party. Problem sorted and it's all good."

I looked at the dress and then took it off the hanger. Dakshima was right – what was I thinking, I had a whole wardrobe of clothes that Jade Caruso would kill for! Leaving them unworn was unthinkable, no matter how much they reminded me of Hollywood.

"You and Anne-Marie are more alike than you think," I said, my voice muffled as I temporarily got my head stuck in an armhole.

"If you say so," Dakshima snorted, pulling the dress over my shoulders. "Nice one," she said, with a nod of approval.

Just then there was a knock at the door and Mum popped her head round it.

"Look who's here," she said, pushing the door back for Nydia, who was wearing a green silk dress with a paler green stole wrapped around her shoulders. She had sprayed her skin with gold glitter spray so that she sparkled.

"Hello," Dakshima said, with a friendly and slightly shy smile.

"You look great," I said. "It's a shame Greg is still up north – he'd be blown away!"

"Thanks," Nydia said, before adding, "I texted him a photo.

"Right, well," Mum said, with the funny look on her face that she usually had when she wanted to hug me but knew I'd drop dead from embarrassment if she did. "Hurry up and get your glad rags on then, girls. I'm dropping you off at Anne-Marie's and Nydia's dad is picking you up at 10.30 sharp, so be ready, no excuses, OK? I want you in this door at 10.45 latest. Dakshima's mum and dad are trusting me to take care of her tonight, so don't let me down."

"We won't," I said, rolling my eyes at the others.

Secretly though I liked having my old un-Hollywood mum back again. Since she started going out with world famous star of stage and screen Jeremy Fort, she kept her roots tinted and her nails manicured and wore high heels on weekdays to go to the supermarket, that was true. But at least the orange skin and stiff face that she had experimented with had faded away, and with it had gone the monster mom she'd become for a while. In Hollywood she'd been so ambitious for me and blinded by the glamour that just for a bit she forgot about asking me what I wanted or how I felt about everything that happened over there. So I didn't mind if she told me off for leaving my shoes in the hall or wiped off the lip-gloss I tried wearing to school with spit on a tissue. That was *my* mum, the one who wanted what was best for me, even if it was sometimes boring and a total lip-gloss-free zone.

With Anne-Marie unavailable, it was Dakshima who did our make-up, me first and then Nydia. Considering jeans and trainers are her favourite things, she seemed like an expert. (It would have been hard to be worse than me. I tried out some pink and purple eye shadow a while back and my Auntie Pat asked me if I had conjunctivitis.)

"You're good at eyeliner," I said, admiring hers, which swished out at the corners making her eyes look even bigger than they were.

"Well, it's the law in my house to learn how to do make-up. My mum started teaching me when I was about three," Dakshima said with a laugh.

"What are you going to wear?" Nydia asked.

"This," Dakshima said uncertainly. "I've got a couple

of dresses but this is the sparkliest most "fabulous" thing I could think of. It's my sister's and if she finds out I've borrowed it I will be dead, so don't let me spill anything on it."

Dakshima held up a two piece Indian trouser suit in a rich deep purple that was decorated with gold thread and beading all around the neck and sleeves.

"Wow!" Nydia said.

"It's a bit more Bollywood than Hollywood," Dakshima said, a little uncertainly.

"It's amazing," Nydia said. "Ooh, this is going to be a good party, I can feel it."

"I hope so," I said, as Mum called us from downstairs. "Otherwise Anne-Marie will never shut up about it."

"Rubes," Nydia laughed, "whether it's the best party in the world or the worst, there is one thing we know for sure…"

The two of us looked at each other and laughed.

"…Anne-Marie will *never* shut up about it."

I was quiet in the car while Nydia gave Dakshima the lowdown on Anne-Marie's place. I was feeling nervous and not only because I'd be seeing all of the Academy kids again for the first time since the Valentine's disco.

I'd be seeing Danny too, and he was bound to be there with Melody. Anne-Marie had told me that despite her policy of inviting everyone she even vaguely knew, whether she liked them or not, she was happy to un-invite Danny and Melody if I wanted her to. And I had wanted her to, but I told her it was fine. I knew that they all still hung out with him at the Academy so it would have been silly for Anne-Marie not to invite him. Besides, I wanted him to see that I didn't care any more, even though that was a total lie; he seemed to be stubbornly sticking around in my head despite my best efforts to get him out of it. Even a Valentine's kiss for Hollywood High hunk Hunter Blake (as *Teen Girl! Magazine* called him) hadn't dislodged Danny from my daydreams, which was highly inconvenient. I decided to try a bit of method acting to see if that worked. I thought if I acted like I didn't give him a second thought for long enough, then pretty soon it would become true.

It was funny that no matter how much I tired to give up acting, there was always a little part of me still doing it.

"Jade is going to be gutted," Nydia said, as Mum pulled the car up outside Anne-Marie's electronic gates and they began to open. "Everyone is going to be talking about this party for weeks and weeks."

She wasn't wrong about that.

When Anne-Marie's dad said she could have anything she wanted for her fourteenth birthday party, he probably hadn't quite expected her to go to the lengths that she did, which is most probably his own fault for not knowing his daughter very well. If he was trying to not feel so guilty by spending a ton of money, then he almost succeeded, except that Anne-Marie wasn't currently speaking to him since he refused to book McFly to play the music.

"Not that he'll notice," she told me on the phone earlier that day. "It's hard to know someone is snubbing you when you're eight thousand miles away."

But even without McFly the party was pretty amazing.

Me, Nydia and Dakshima were open mouthed as Mum drove us up to the front door. "Maybe I should have hired a limo," she said, laughing nervously as we coasted along the driveway. It was lined with huge spotlights that sent shafts of light up into the night sky and must have been visible for miles around. "A clapped out Corsa doesn't quite seem like the right ride for such an occasion."

The whole house (and it's really more of a mansion) was covered in fairy lights that twinkled and sparkled. We said goodbye to Mum and walked in through the front door where a snooty looking man in a bow tie and tails took our coats, while another one dressed in exactly the same way offered a fruit juice cocktail.

"You're telling me that most of the time only three people live in this house?" Dakshima whispered in my ear as we headed towards the ballroom. "That's wild!"

"It is a bit mad, isn't it?" I said. "But I bet you'd rather have your mum and dad around every day more than a load of money and presents."

"Oh, I don't know," Dakshima said, sipping her strawberry crush.

"Rubes! Nydia! The other one!"

We heard Anne-Marie call out to us as she flew down the staircase (which was brave considering her high heels), flung her arms around me and Nydia, and kissed us on the cheek. "You two look *great*," she said.

"So do you," I said, wiping her lipstick off Nydia with my thumb. She was wearing a silver-sequin covered dress that reached the ankles and pair of matching silver heels that I only had to look at to feel dizzy. I was almost certain that Anne-Marie had been pacing the length of her rather large bedroom for several days perfecting her walk in them. She never left details to chance when it came to her image.

"Great party," Dakshima said, a little awkwardly. "Thanks for inviting me."

"Thanks for coming," Anne-Marie replied stiffly. "I like your outfit. My mum says that Indian style is where it's at this season."

"Right, well," Dakshima said. "Happy Birthday and that."

For a second or two the four of us stood there looking at each other, then Anne-Marie tossed her blonde curls and put her arm through Dakshima's. "Come and meet my boyfriend Sean Rivers," she said. "You have to see him in a tuxedo. If I get him back into acting again he'll make a perfect young James Bond!"

Dakshima glanced back at me as Anne-Marie led her off, but she couldn't resist the chance to meet the hero of *The Underdogs*.

The ballroom was decorated with hundreds of silver stars hanging from the ceiling and a thick red carpet had been laid over the marble floor. I could see Sean by the food, stuffing tiny canapé after tiny canapé into his mouth while laughing with Danny. Sean did look handsome in his suit, but then he always did. Sean's good looks had never seemed to affect me, but the sight of Danny with his hair gelled, looking just as James Bondish, made my tummy flip. I sighed. This method acting lark was much harder than I imagined. I watched as Dakshima nodded her coolest, least bothered hello to Sean and then to Danny. I wanted to go over. I wanted to say hello to Sean because I hadn't seen him in ages, but Danny was there so I stood rooted to the spot wondering where Melody was.

"She's in the loo," Nydia said, reading my mind. "Anne-Marie said she could probably get one of the waiters to lock her in if you want her to. She said she has about twenty toilets so no one would notice."

"Danny would notice." I laughed at the thought of it.

"Really?" Nydia said, looking at Danny messing about with Sean. "I'm not so sure. He doesn't seem to be missing her now."

"Anyway," I said, "I don't care about Danny and Smelody any more. I told you – I'm fully over him."

"Of course you are," Nydia said. "And Anne-Marie bought that dress at Primark."

"I just said hi to the actual Sean Rivers," Dakshima said, her eyes wide, as she came back over to where we were standing. "Sean Rivers stuffing a mini spring roll in his gob and like an ordinary idiot, just like any other boy."

Nydia and I laughed. "That's Sean," I said. "He *is* just like any other boy."

"I haven't got posters of any other boy all over my room," Dakshima said, then clapped her hand over her mouth as she let that detail slip. "Not that I'm that into him or anything."

Nydia and I laughed. "In a minute," Nydia said, "he'll start burping his way through Danny's number one and I promise you, after that you'll totally think he's just like any other boy. Loud, immature and disgusting!"

Nydia and I grinned at each other as we watched Anne-Marie beckon Dakshima back over to her and Sean. "They might even get on after all," I said to Nydia.

"Anything's possible," Nydia said. "Dakshima's great."

"Yeah," I said, laughing as Dakshima's jaw dropped and I wondered if Sean was burping already.

"But she's not like... you know, your new best friend, is she?" Nydia asked carefully.

I stared. "No! No way. I mean, I really like her and everything, and it's good to have a friend at Highgate Comp, but you're my best friend forever, Nyds." I hugged her hard.

"Just checking," Nydia said, as I squeezed. "I don't want to lose you completely."

"Impossible," I told her.

"So, tell me about Highgate then," Nydia said. "Are there any cute boys?"

"Not that I've noticed," I told her, which was true. I knew the boys in the choir – Rohan, Gabe and the others – but I didn't fancy any of them.

"What do you do there? Have you joined a drama group?"

"Well, I've..." I started to tell Nydia about the choir, but then I stopped myself. I knew that she would be sweet and supportive and that really there was no reason not to tell her. But I was pretty sure that even with Adele, Talitha and Hannah in our choir we were too inexperienced and too under-rehearsed to stand a chance of making it to the TV performance. There would be thousands of people auditioning for the leads when we were singing for the school choir competition. If I kept my head down, stood at the back and didn't do anything to get myself noticed, no one from the Academy need ever know I was there. If some of the other girls found out – like Jade, who at that moment walked in through the door, along with Menakshi – then they would make it seem stupid, silly and desperate. I didn't want them to do that. Especially not in front of Dakshima.

"I've... thought about joining a club," I said to cover my tracks. "There's a book club. I might join that."

"Great," Nydia said, confused. She put her hand on my shoulder. "Are you really OK about Danny and Melody now? Because you can tell me if you're not, you know."

"Of course I am," I said, producing a great big smile

that felt like it stretched from one side of my face to the other. "Danny and me splitting up was *weeks* ago – and don't forget I've been kissed by Hunter Blake since then. And anyway, I'm not interested in boys right now."

"None at all?" Nydia asked.

"None at all," I said firmly, glancing over at Danny who was laughing with Melody. "There's more to life than boys and acting and auditioning for musicals, you know."

"Yes, but none of them are half as much fun." I felt my tummy lurch as Jade Caruso butted in to our conversation. "How nice to see you again, Ruby. Are you out of rehab now?"

"Jade, you know perfectly well I wasn't in rehab," I said heavily. "I had a bit of time off of school because I was tired, that's all."

"Oh so that thing in *Hiya! Bye-a!* about nervous exhaustion wasn't true then?"

"No it wasn't," I said, looking around for an escape route. "Congratulations on the musical, by the way. Sounds like it's going to be great."

"It is," Jade said, winking at Menakshi. "Stage schools all over the country are auditioning for the leads, including everyone at the Academy. Hundreds of people will be lining up for a chance and I'll be one of them.

Shame that you've given up, Ruby. Still, the competition would be very tough so perhaps it's better. You wouldn't want any more 'nervous exhaustion', would you?"

"Jade, you are such a cow," Nydia said.

"At least I don't look like one," Jade said, turning on her heel and walking away.

"I'm gonna..."

Nydia held my arm as I started off after Jade, ready for a fight. "Don't let her get to you," she said. "I shouldn't have called her a cow. I'll never get a part in the musical now, not if she's got anything to do with it."

"I'm sure Jade hasn't got any say, not really," I tried to reassure Nydia. "She's just making out that she has to wield power over all of you. I could just thump her, I really— Oh, hi, Danny." I turned around to find my ex-boyfriend smiling at me, that sweet half smile he did whenever he thought I'd said something funny. "How are you?"

I sounded like I'd just sucked the air out of one of the million or so helium balloons that were dotted about the place.

"Hi, Danny," Nydia said. "I'm just going to go and... go over there – bye!"

Danny and I looked at each other. "I'm OK," he said. "I just thought I'd come and say hi."

"Really?" I said, wishing I hadn't sounded quite so surprised.

"Yeah," Danny added. "So – hi, er, how are you? How's the new school?"

"It's great actually," I said, making myself smile at him and trying to remember my method acting.

"So you're happy then?" he said.

"Very," I said. Method acting was turning out to be a lot harder than I thought it would be.

"And how about what's-his-name, that bloke... Hunter Blake?" he said, sort of coughing out the name.

"He's great too," I said, choosing not to mention that I hadn't heard from Hunter since he'd gone back to Hollywood.

"Great," Danny said.

"Great," I said.

We looked at each other for a moment longer and then he said, "Ruby... I..."

"Yes?"

"It's just that..."

"What?"

"Well...."

"Oh, Danny, if you've got something to say, just say it!" I snapped.

"You've got lipstick on your cheek," Danny said.

"Looks like Anne-Marie's."

He walked off, leaving me standing alone at the party. *So much for cool and aloof*, I thought to myself.

"Take that back!" I looked round to find Dakshima face to face with Jade, and it didn't look as if they were getting on. "I *said*, take that back," Dakshima repeated.

"Don't be ridiculous," Jade said. "Who *are* you anyway?"

"What's going on?" I asked, running over to join them.

"She told me she was the one whose dad's doing the musical, so I told her about the choir and us going in for the competition, and she said a school like ours would never get through. She said we might as well not even bother to enter."

"I'm only being honest," Jade said with a shrug. "Schools from all over the country are entering – what chance does a rat hole like Highgate Comp have?"

"As much chance as anyone," I protested.

"We're just as good as any other choir," Dakshima said, making a pretty bold claim considering we'd only had one rehearsal so far and only about five of us could actually sing. Dakshima looked at me. "Aren't we, Ruby?"

I winced and braced myself.

"*We?*" Jade said archly looking at me, as if she were

sharpening her talons for the kill. "Ruby, are you in this pathetic little choir?"

"*Are* you, Rubes?" Nydia asked.

"Yes," I said uncomfortably. "I have to be in it, it was compulsory…"

"This is hilarious," Jade screeched. "Ruby Parker, Hollywood Star, reduced to joining some grubby little school choir to try and get her life back. You're career is over, Ruby. Deal with it."

"I know it is," I said. "I didn't even want to be in the choir—"

"Ruby!" Dakshima protested, her eyes wide.

"Well, I'm sorry, Dakshima, you know I didn't," I said. "I knew exactly what would happen – people would think I'd made a mistake leaving the Academy and that I was trying to get back into show business. But I didn't. I joined because I had to. And I know we aren't going to win, and after it is all over and I will be able to go back to the life I want."

"Good job," Jade said. "The last thing the world of entertainment needs is more Ruby Parker."

"Knock it off, Jade," Sean said casually. "Don't talk about Ruby like that."

Jade eyed Sean up and down. "One washed-up child star protecting another one. How sweet. Are you sure you shouldn't be jealous, Anne-Marie?"

"Jade Caruso," Anne-Marie said, "I knew I shouldn't have invited you to this party. I don't care who your dad is, or how many musicals he's launching, you can't come into my house and speak to my friends that way. As of this minute I'm *un*inviting you. Goodbye."

"You can't do that," Jade said furiously as the other guests gathered round to watch the action.

"Door's that way," Anne-Marie said, nodding in the general direction of the exit.

"You're throwing me out of your party because of *her*?" Jade seethed, gesturing at me, "This is a big mistake, Anne-Marie…"

"The big mistake was inviting you in the first place," Anne-Marie said, her smile as sharp as broken glass. "I don't know what I was thinking. I must have had a temporary brain by-pass. Better than the permanent lack of talent you've got though, hey, Jade?"

"You've just lost any chance you had of getting a part in *Spotlight!* now!" Jade shouted, making the other guests gasp. "It's my dad and my musical, and you won't get anywhere near it."

"Not bothered," Anne-Marie said. "Because unlike you, Jade, I don't need my daddy to get a part in a show. I can get it on my own. Do pick up a party bag on the way out."

Jade looked around at the Academy kids. "If you want a shot at *Spotlight!* you'd better come with me now," she said.

There was silence as everyone looked at each other.

"Come on then!" Jade said, walking out. After a moment, a few of the other kids followed her. Michael Henderson, Menakshi and her usual cronies, but also some of the other kids. They didn't even look at Anne-Marie as they went.

"Come on, Danny," I heard Melody speak from behind me.

Danny stood his ground. "I'm not going," he said. "Anne-Marie is my friend. I'm not ditching her."

"But the musical," Melody said. "What about the musical?"

"Melody," Danny said firmly, "I'm not going."

Melody dropped his hand and then walked up to Anne-Marie. "Look, I'm sorry, but..."

"See ya," Anne-Marie said brightly, waving her hand.

Along with Melody, about half of the guests had followed Jade, leaving the glittering ballroom still and silent.

"I thought you Brits were supposed to be steadfast and loyal," Sean said, holding Anne-Marie's hand.

"Not when it comes to fighting over the chance to

play a lead part in a musical it seems," Anne-Marie said quietly before mustering a smile. "Anyway, who cares? Everyone who's gone was rank anyway..." Catching Danny's eye she added, "Well, you know what I mean. Thanks for staying, Danny."

"You know she'll do her best to ruin the *Spotlight!* auditions for you now, don't you?" Danny asked her with a shrug.

"Well, she can try," Anne-Marie said, hugging me briefly. "But she won't succeed. True talent like mine can't be hidden. Come on, everybody. Let's dance!

It was almost time to go home when Sean found me in the corner watching the remaining guests dance. "You should dance," he told me, catching his breath. "That Dakshima girl can really move!"

"I don't know," I said, watching Danny do his moves on the dance floor. He wasn't really a dancer, but he'd had to learn a routine for the video of his single and he kept repeating that over and over again, no matter what the track. "I'm not really in the mood."

"The Academy isn't the same without you around," Sean said, leaning against the wall and grinning at me. "We haven't had a surprise visit from a movie star recently and no one's run off to Hollywood in weeks."

"I bet that's not true," I said, returning his smile. "I bet you had three Oscar winners in last week."

"Well maybe," Sean said, looking thoughtful. "Ruby, I know I said I get why you left and everything, but, well, I remember you telling me not so long ago that you can't ever really give up something that is so much a part of you. You told me that I was an actor through and through and that I couldn't change that. You're why I decided to go to the Academy, instead of giving up acting for good."

"Yes, but you're *brilliant* at it, Sean. You're a true star," I told him. "I'm just average, even below average probably. Giving up is the right thing for me."

"Would it make any difference if I told you I didn't think that was true? That I thought you were brilliant too?" Sean asked me.

"If you do think that, then every single critic and producer in Hollywood disagrees with you," I told him with a sad smile.

"Well, if there's one thing I learnt in Hollywood," Sean replied, "it's that those guys? They don't know a thing."

Dakshima was very quiet in Nydia's dad's car on the way home and when we were dropped back at mine she paused on the front step. "I don't know about sleeping over, Ruby," she said. "Might go home, if you don't mind."

"But why?" I asked. "I thought we had fun tonight."

"We did," Dakshima said. "The party was really cool after that Jade left, and even Anne-Marie's OK once you get to know her. It's just that... I don't think you really want to be at our school. And if you don't really want to be at our school, then you can't really want to be real friends, with me, Talitha, Hannah or any of the others."

"What do you mean?" I asked her. "Of course I want to be at Highgate. I chose it!"

"You're embarrassed about being in the choir and about going in for the competition with us," Dakshima said. "You didn't even tell your best friends about it! Seems like being at Highgate is just a game for you. Maybe when you get bored hanging around with kids like me, you can get mummy to pack you back to stage school again, but for us it's real. Our school really needs to win that money, Ruby, and now everyone in the choir is trying really hard because of you. You inspired us. I thought that you were one of us now, but you're not really. I don't think you could be even if you wanted to be. So I think I'd rather go home."

"I *am* one of you," I said. "I'm sorry, Dakshima. You're right, I *was* embarrassed about being in the choir, but you saw what Jade is like. I knew she'd laugh at me. And I'll be honest with you, I don't think the choir has a chance of winning the *Spotlight!* competition. But I do care, I really do. And I want to help the choir get as far as it can."

"Really?" Dakshima asked me. "Because if anyone can help it's you."

"They won't put us through just because I used to be famous," I told her.

"No, that's not what I meant," Dakshima said. "You know about theatre, you know how to act a song, how to get us to stand so we look good – you can even tell us what to wear for the audition. Ruby, you can make a difference to the choir because you know all of those things."

"Really?" I said thoughtfully. "Do you really think so?"

"Well there's only one way to prove it, isn't there," Dakshima said.

"What that?" I asked her.

"Help make the choir so good that even Jade won't be able to stand in our way," Dakshima said.

"Alone in a Crowd"
Words and Music by *Mick Caruso*

All my friends are around me

Everyone here thinks I'm so great

And I know that I should be happy

But happiness will have to wait

Because until I find you...

I'm alone in a crowd

Unless I have you holding my hand

I'm alone in crowd

Unless you can understand

That I love you so much I want to sing it out loud

But I can't... no I can't, because I'm alone in a crowd

Without you

Another handshake, a clap on the back

Another kiss on the cheek

Another compliment, a round of applause

Can't they see I'm lost and weak?

Because until I find you...

I'm alone in a crowd

Without you my heart can't beat

I'm alone in crowd

I don't even want to eat

They all think I'm feeling happy and proud

But I can't… no I can't, because I'm alone in a crowd

Without you

And suddenly, there you are standing in the doorway

Your smile is brighter than the star on my

dressing room door

And when you push your way through the crowd

to stand before me

I know that I am not alone in a crowd any more

Not alone in a crowd,

Now that I've got you with me

Not alone in a crowd

Because you complete me

And I know that when you're standing by my side

There's no fear, no nothing left to hide

When I have you

Chapter Six

"Right now, people, put the sandwiches away please," Mr Petrelli said. "Even with extra after school rehearsals we need all the time we've got, so less eating and more singing."

"I'm starving, sir," Gabe said, reluctantly putting his Mars bar back in his bag.

"And me," Talitha said. "I need my carbohydrates, sir, otherwise I get faint."

"I'm sure you do, Talitha," Mr Petrelli said. "Ten more minutes then we'll finish for today, but we need to do something to improve *Alone in a Crowd*. It seems so flat – and I don't mean the singing. It's got no sparkle or... pizzazz."

"Pizzazz, sir?" Gabe said, looking at Rohan. "Isn't that a type of microwavable rice?"

"Funny, Gabe," Mr Petrelli said. "I just can't seem to put my finger on the problem..."

Dakshima elbowed me in the ribs. "Ouch!" I said, scowling at her.

"Ruby might have an idea, sir," Dakshima said. "She knows all about this sort of thing after all."

Every one looked at me.

"That's true, Dakshima. We should make the best use of our assets. Any ideas, Ruby?"

I stared hard at Dakshima, but my "I'm gonna get you" glare can't have been that scary because she just grinned back at me.

"Um, well…" I said, looking at Mr Petrelli and then back down at the lyrics sheet. "This song isn't really supposed to be for the chorus, is it? It's Arial Logan's big solo, so maybe that's why it isn't working. With all of us singing it together, we don't exactly give the impression of being alone in a crowd, do we?" Mr Petrelli was frowning quite hard. "Or maybe not. After all, what do I know?"

"No, you're right," Mr Petrelli said after a moment, breaking into a smile. "Completely right. This *is* a solo – but we have to sing it for the audition. All the schools do. So how can we make it work?"

"Well…" I began uncertainly, an idea beginning to form in my mind.

"Go on, Ruby," Mr Petrelli said.

I glanced around, everyone was looking at me again. "Well, we could try and stage the song a bit more," I suggested. "Instead of us all standing in three rows singing, we could stand apart, with spaces in between us. And we could have solos – get the strongest singers Adele, Talitha, Hannah and Dakshima to sing a verse each. And maybe as one soloist finishes their bit, they could walk over and touch the next one on the arm, like they are passing the loneliness and the song on. Sort of a singing relay. And it would be a bit more of a show then, because it's a chorus they need and not a school choir."

There was a moment's silence and everyone looked at Mr Petrelli.

"I like it," Mr Petrelli said. "Girls, are you happy to sing solo?

"In front of everyone?" Adele asked him nervously.

"Yes, Adele," Mr Petrelli said. "In fact with your voice I think I might get you to start."

"No, sir, I can't," Adele said, anxiously. "I'm really sorry. I love singing, but I can't do it on my own. If you make me do that in front of the judges I'll crack, I know I will."

"You might not," I said, clapping her on the back. "Come on, Adele, you've got the best voice here!"

"Thanks, Ruby, but I still can't, and I don't want to mess it up for everyone else. Please, sir, don't make me."

Mr Petrelli looked thoughtful. "Of course we won't make you, Adele."

"I've got no problem with going first," Talitha said.

"I'll go second," Hannah added.

"Don't mind when I go," Dakshima said.

"Well, this a girl's song, so we need another girl. Next on my list of singers will have to be... Ruby Parker."

"Me?" I said, clapping my hand on my chest. "You want me to sing on my *own*?"

"Yes, Ruby, I didn't pick you to be in the choir just to torture you. You have a nice voice," Mr Petrelli said. "You need to find a bit more confidence and strength, but out of everyone here you have the most experience in performing. And as it was your idea to stage the song, it seems only fair you get some of the spotlight, excuse the pun... again."

"I don't want the spotlight," I said. "I'm very happy in the shadows, me."

"Come on, Ruby, you're part of a team remember," Dakshima said. "We need you."

"Yeah, come on, Ruby," Gabe and Talitha said together.

"Give it a go," Rohan said.

"Just because I used to be on TV and in films and things – well, it doesn't mean I'd be any better on a stage performing live. I've never done that," I told them.

"Let's try it," Mr Petrelli said. "Dakshima, Talitha, Hannah and then Ruby – and all join in on the last verse.

Let's run it through now and I'll come up with some backing harmonies for the rest of you. Ready? Five, six, seven, eight..."

Standing completely still, I listened as the other girls began to sing their parts. Every muscle in my body clenched and I knew that this was a terrible idea. I might sound OK as part of the choir, but on my own I'd be awful, I just knew it. I mean, I didn't even sing into my hairbrush in front of the mirror. I didn't even sing at a performing arts school – *that's* how bad a singer I was.

I looked over at Dakshima who was singing her heart out and knew it was my turn next. She'd said she thought I didn't want to be part of the school, that I didn't want to try, but she was wrong. I even wanted to be part of the choir, especially after Jade was so rude about us. I wanted to show Jade and everybody that you don't have to go to a posh stage school to succeed and that Highgate Comp is just as good as any other school.

The only thing left for me to do was to try. *And then, I thought, when they realise that I really am awful, at least they will see that I tried and nobody will hate me.*

I took a deep breath as Dakshima came over, touched my arm and I sang.

* * *

"Brilliant," Mr Petrelli said, clapping his hands together as we all finished together. "You were all brilliant and – Ruby, where did that voice come from? You've been hiding it from me all this time."

"Have I?" I said, looking around at the others, who clapped me on the back and told me well done.

"OK, OK, settle down," Mr Petrelli said as the girls hugged each other and the boys tried not to look like they cared either way. "We've still got a lot of work to do. We need to tighten up the harmonies on *Spotlight*, work out some backing harmonies for *Alone in a Crowd* and this is our last rehearsal. So less patting each other on the back and more singing. And Ruby, if you have any other ideas, let me know, because I've got a feeling we might just pull this off!"

I looked around at Dakshima, Talitha, Hannah, Adele, Gurkay, Gabe and the rest of Highgate Comprehensive choir and suddenly I felt like I really belonged to something for the first time in a long time.

And it was funny really, because until then I hadn't realised that it was me who'd been feeling alone in a crowd all along.

When we came out of school, we were all laughing and talking. Talitha was pretending that she wasn't deliberately trying to walk next to Gabe when everybody could tell that she was, and Dakshima and Hannah were practising their harmonies. I was surprised to see my mum sitting in her car waiting for me. She hadn't picked me up from school since I started walking home with Dakshima.

"Do you want a lift?" I asked Dakshima, waving at my mum, who grinned and waved back.

"You mum looks really happy," Talitha said. "Why is that?"

"She's in love," I said, grimacing. "She's been happy all the time since she started going out with Jeremy Fort."

"A happy mum is better than a miserable one," Hannah reminded me.

"I'm going to walk," Dakshima told me. "See you tomorrow!"

"And good luck with your happy mother," Talitha added.

"Hi, Mum," I said, opening the passenger door and sliding in next to her.

"Hello, love. How was your day?" Mum asked, flinging her arms around me and kissing me on the cheek.

"Same as usual," I said warily. "Mum, what's happened? Why are you so... hyper?"

"Hyper? Am I?" Mum laughed happily. "We've got a surprise visitor."

I looked at her shining eyes. "Jeremy?" I asked, even though it was obvious from all the soppiness and the fact that she was wearing lipstick at five in the afternoon. Jeremy was filming in Hungary and we hadn't seen him for nearly a month. He phoned a lot, but I knew that she still missed him.

"Yes," Mum said happily. "He landed this morning, says he's got a week off and he wants to spend it with us."

"With you, more like," I said, and I wasn't upset; it was just the truth.

"With us *both*," Mum insisted. "He's got something to tell us apparently.

"Really?" I looked sideways at my mum. "Like what?"

"I don't know," Mum said. "He wanted to wait for you to get back from school. It's probably whether or not we would like to go on holiday with him for a bit, or visit him on set in Hungary. Or maybe he's got a new film role."

"Hmmmm," I said. "Maybe."

"Ruby!" Jeremy greeted me with a big hug when I came in, standing up so that Everest had to scramble off his lap to safety. "I was just getting reacquainted with your cat. I think he was after my breath mints. David misses you, you know. He hasn't been the same since you left us."

David was the scrawny little Chihuahua that Jeremy rescued from some starlet who had abandoned the dog when he wasn't fashionable any more. At first I hadn't really liked the animal, with his needley little teeth and bony body, and I think he felt more or less the same way about me. But by the end of my stay in Hollywood, we were pretty good friends, even if it was because nobody else seemed to likes us much.

"So how's the new school?" Jeremy asked.

"It's great actually," I said. "I'm in the choir. I sang a solo today and I didn't completely suck, and on Sunday we're going in for this competition where the winners get to be part of the chorus of a show. We won't win, which is shame because we need the prize money more than anything."

"You're singing a solo?" Mum asked me in disbelief.

"I know," I said. "Mr Petrelli said it was good. But I went to the Academy for all of those years and no one ever discovered my singing voice there, so I don't think it can be *that* good, do you? Which is another reason I don't think we'll win."

"Sounds like you haven't completely given up on show business altogether then?" Jeremy asked me.

"I have," I said. "I've given up on people following me around and writing mean and untrue things about me and my family when they don't even know me. But I quite like being the choir. It's surprisingly fun."

"I'm glad you're happy," Jeremy said, suddenly looking rather nervous. "I've something I wanted to tell you and your mother."

"Really?" I said. "Are you offering me a new film project? Because I'm not accepting any roles. I've turned down two since we got back from Hollywood. One was a Japanese martial arts film, and one about a school prefect who discovers she can fly."

"No," Jeremy said glancing at my mum. "It's not about work, it's more about... home. I wanted to ask both of you if you thought it would be OK... by which I mean a good idea, if I were to move back to London permanently?"

"Really?" My mum clasped her hands together. "You'd be living in London?"

"Yes, if you're amenable to the idea," Jeremy said, beaming at my mother who was clearly about as amenable as a person possibly could be. "I'm tired of film making and I miss the buzz of live theatre. I've been offered the post of creative director at the Harlequin in the West End. I'm going to take it. I'll bring Augusto, Marie and David with me too, of course. And best of all, I'll be near all of the people I care about," he looked at me. "By which I mean you and your mother, Ruby."

"Oh, Jeremy, that's wonderful news," Mum said happily.

"It's great," I said. "And of course we will."

"Of course you will what?" Jeremy asked me.

"Help you buy a house!" I told him. "How much money have you got? Do you want a ballroom because those houses are quite pricey, we'll need to know how many loos, bedrooms, a swimming pool..."

"Oh, right," Jeremy said. "I see, I hadn't thought – what do you think?"

"I think a ballroom is really handy for parties," I told him. "And at your age you need all the exercise you can get, so a swimming pool is a must."

"I'm going to be in Hungary for the next few weeks," Jeremy told me, "so I think I'll leave the details up to you. Just find me a house somewhere near here that both of you really like. Because if you like it, then it truly will be a home."

"Oh, Jeremy," Mum sighed.

"That was so corny," I said. "Is that a line from a film?"

And we all laughed, except Everest, who was still searching for Jeremy's mints.

Later that evening, after Jeremy had made us all lasagne for tea and I was lying on my bed trying to do my maths homework, Mum came up to see me.

"Ruby?" she called my name quietly on the other side of my bedroom door.

"Come in," I said, glad of an excuse to put my books away for a minute.

"How's it going?" Mum said, sitting on the edge of the bed.

"Fine," I said. "Maths, you know. Bleugh."

"I didn't mean with you homework…" Mum hesitated. "I meant with you. Are you OK about everything?"

I blinked at her and sat up. "Yes," I said, and then just to be on the safe side. "OK about what?"

"It's just the last time I thought you were really happy and fine about things, I got it completely wrong and you ran away in the middle of the night and put yourself in terrible danger. So I just wanted to check, to see if you're worried anything. About Jeremy moving to London. About me and Jeremy becoming closer. If any of that makes you feel uncomfortable, sad or angry, then I want you to tell me so that we can talk about it."

I made a note to myself to never EVER run away in middle of night after stealing my mum's credit cards to book flight across the Atlantic ever EVER again. All it really achieved was Mum worrying about me far too much, far too often, and when she really didn't have to. And a lot of intense conversations while she tried to work out if I was having a nervous breakdown or not.

"Do you mean am I upset that Jeremy is moving to London to be closer to you?" I asked. Mum nodded, a frown slotted between her brows.

"No, of course not," I told her. "I'm glad he'll be around more. You and he might be... you know, a couple and that, but he's my friend too, Mum. Don't forget he was my friend before you two even got together. And it will be cool to see David again, the scrawny mutt. Plus when Jeremy's around, you're all happy and shiny and I get away with a lot more stuff."

"Like what?" My mum asked me laughing.

"Like being able to wear just a tiny bit of clear lip-gloss to school in the morning like almost all the other girls do?" I asked her quickly, hopeful that her happiness would make her relent.

"No, Ruby," Mum said mildly, standing up and leaning over to kiss me. "No make-up to school."

"Just a tiny, tiny bit," I pleaded. "You'd hardly know it was there!"

"Nope," Mum said, going to the door. "Now get on with your homework.

"Mum-um," I protested, letting my head flop down on to the bed.

"Oh and Rube?" Mum said, making me lift my head so

my hair flopped all over my face. "I'm so proud of you, now more than ever."

I looked up, then smiled. "I know you and Jeremy are in love, but you have got to stop being so soppy," I told her. "It's ruining my cred."

Mum was laughing as she closed the door.

SPOTLIGHT! THE MUSICAL ©
Produced by Caruso Carousel Productions
In conjunction with Bright Young Things TV

The Spotlight! School Choir Competition©
Rules for Competitors

1. All choirs must be pre-registered by their teachers at least two weeks before the regional heats.

2. The names of choir members must be submitted at the time of registration. New members are not permitted to join after the commencement of the competition.

3. Choir members may not also participate in the SPOTLIGHT!: SEARCH FOR A STAR© (Produced by BYT-TV)

4. Parents and guardians of all choir members must give their consent for their child/children to appear on SPOTLIGHT!: SEARCH FOR A STAR THE FINAL© (Produced by BYT-TV) before the competition commences.

5. Parents and guardians must give their consent for their child/children to appear in the live televised premiere of SPOTLIGHT! THE MUSICAL©.

6. All choirs must sing the songs that have been chosen for them.

7. All choirs must be amateur choirs affiliated with the school and receive no professional training outside of the school.

8. The *SPOTLIGHT! SCHOOL CHOIR COMPETITION©* believes in equal opportunities for all and fair play. Any choir deemed to be going against the spirit of the competition will be eliminated.

Enjoy the competition and Good Luck!

Chapter Seven

It was Saturday morning, the day before the auditions, when Anne-Marie and Nydia came up with the best idea they have ever had. Me, Anne-Marie, Nydia and Dakshima had gone to a café for hot chocolate. At least Nydia, Dakshima and I were having hot chocolate.

"You're having an espresso?" I asked Anne-Marie as a tiny cup of strong black coffee was placed in front of her.

"I am," Anne-Marie said airily. "I'm fourteen now, Rubes. I have sophisticated tastes."

"What, just like that, overnight, you stopped liking sweet, milky, chocolatey drinks topped off with whipped cream and a flake, and started to like small, hot, dark bitter ones?" Nydia and I grinned at each other.

"Actually, I've liked espressos for ages and I fancy one this morning," Anne-Marie said. "It's no big deal. Honestly, you thirteen-year-olds are *so* immature."

"Are you telling me that after my birthday in a few weeks' time I'll be necking coffee?" Dakshima asked her.

Anne-Marie raised an eyebrow. "Sophisticated tastes

99

come with more than age," she said archly, but with a twinkle in her eye.

"Thank goodness for that," Dakshima said. "Coffee is rank, man."

I took a big slurp of my chocolate so that it left a whipped-cream moustache on my top lip and grinned at Anne-Marie. "Drink up then," I said, nodding at the espresso.

Anne-Marie looked at the tiny little cup. "I'm waiting for it to cool down," she said, making the rest of us collapse into giggles. "I am!" She protested, trying not to laugh. "It's very hot!"

"Tell us more about Jeremy moving to London, Ruby." Nydia said. "Do you think he is going to ask your mum to marry him?"

"I don't think so," I said. "I suppose he might one day, but not yet. Mum called Dad and told him about the move last night, but I'm not seeing him until he takes me to the choir competition tomorrow so I don't really know how he feels about it. I shouldn't think he'll mind though. And today Mum and Jeremy are going to look at houses. They're going to rule out all of the rubbish ones and then call me in for an opinion when they've got a shortlist."

"To think that Jeremy Fort fancies your mum," Nydia said. "You can see that he really, *really* loves her like mad."

"It's so romantic," Anne-Marie said wistfully. "And so A-list."

"What really worries *me*," I said, keen to change the subject, "is the competition tomorrow." I looked at Dakshima. "It's going to be really tough."

"Ruby Parker, choir member," Anne-Marie said. "Now that *is* a turn up. No offence, Dakshima, but your choir must be awful if Ruby's one of the best."

"She can sing," Dakshima protested. "It's just that in a school full of singers nobody noticed. Mr Petrelli says she will be really good if she works at it."

"Really?" Even Nydia sounded disbelieving.

"It doesn't matter anyway," I said. "Because we are not going to win and my singing career will be over before it began."

"I reckon we're going to win," Dakshima said with a shrug.

"How do you work that out?" I asked her. "We only formed the choir a couple of weeks ago, we've got less experience, less talent and less... everything than probably any other choir that's entering."

"So?" Dakshima said. "Aren't you forgetting my favourite film?"

I looked blank.

"*The Underdogs*?" Dakshima reminded me. She looked

at Nydia and Anne-Marie. "You've all seen it right?"

"Only about a million times," Anne-Marie said. "Did I mention that my boyfriend is in that film?"

"Only about a million times," Nydia said.

"What does Sean's character say in it?" Dakshima went on. "*If a little person has a big enough heart, then anything is possible.*"

"That film is so bad," Anne-Marie said. "But Dakshima's right. It's possible. Unlikely, but possible."

"Anyway," I said, keen not to think about me singing solo in front of a panel of judges. "Are you two ready for tomorrow?"

The auditions to find the finalists for the lead parts were on the same day as the choir competition, in the same West End conference centre.

"I am," Anne-Marie said, still not touching her coffee. "I'm going to sing 'There's a Place for Us' from *West Side Story*. I'm going to wear a black T-shirt, a red skirt and a red scarf round my neck like they did in the olden days."

"I'm doing 'Hopelessly Devoted to You' from *Grease*," Nydia said. "I borrowed a Pink Ladies jacket that my next door neighbour had from a school play."

"Aren't you dying with nerves?" Dakshima asked them both.

Anne-Marie shook her head. "I don't get nerves. If you've prepared as much as you possibly can and you know you have talent, what is there to be nervous about?"

"Pooing in your pants?" Dakshima said, making us all laugh.

"I get nervous," Nydia said. "But I think that after Anne-Marie's party and the way she threw Jade and her friends out of it, there's no chance that either of us are going to get through to the finals, so I'm just going to relax and enjoy myself."

"That Jade girl can't run the whole thing," Dakshima said. "She's just a kid. Her dad's not crazy, is he? He won't give all the parts to her friends just because she says so?"

"Maybe not," Anne-Marie said. "But what Jade wants Jade usually gets."

"Serious? My dad won't even let me have a Nintendo DS," Dakshima exclaimed miserably.

"I know how you feel," Anne-Marie said. "My dad wouldn't even let me have McFly – how tight is that?"

"So what are you lot wearing?" Nydia asked me and Dakshima.

"Our uniforms," Dakshima said with a shrug.

"Your *school* uniforms?"

"Yep, that's what Mr Petrelli said," I told Nydia. "Clean, ironed uniforms."

"*Every* choir is going to be wearing their uniforms!" Anne-Marie exclaimed. "You want to stand out. You need to show them that you are more than a choir – you're a chorus, ready for live theatre!"

"But costumes?" I asked her, sceptical. "We don't get to sing what we like, like you two. We have to sing three songs from the show."

"So *Spotlight!* is set in a stage school," Anne-Marie replied. "Wear a stage school costume."

"What, like the Academy uniform, you mean?" I asked, feeling confused.

"No, dummy, like... dance wear. You know – leg warmers, headbands, lycra, the lot. Then you'll stick out a mile and they'll see that you're more than just singers – you're performers."

"I'm not sure I like the sound of sticking out a mile," I said.

"Plus Mr Petrelli never said anything about costumes," Dakshima said uncertainly. "Can you imagine getting Gabe into dance wear? It ain't gonna happen."

"Not to mention, where on earth would we find twelve dance outfits for boys and girls by tomorrow?" I added.

"In my wardrobe, of course," Anne-Marie said. "Daddy might not have let me have McFly, but he knows how much I like a leotard."

"And what about the boys?" I asked her, incredulous.

"My brother did ballet for ten years," Anne-Marie said. "He's still got all the kit in his room. So round up your team and get them over to mine. I'll have you all kitted out in no time, even this Gabe bloke."

I looked at Dakshima. "What do you think?"

"I think we haven't asked Mr Petrelli," Dakshima said.

Anne-Marie leant a little closer and said. "Come on, Dakshima, live a little. Take a risk – or are you too scared?"

Dakshima bit her lip for a second and then a slow smile spread across her face. "OK," she said. "I will if you will. Drink that coffee and you've got a deal."

At first I didn't think the others would go for it. In fact, as Dakshima and I called everyone, we were sure that they would all say no. Then Dakshima told them if they agreed to meet us at Anne-Marie's house, there was quite good chance they'd meet Sean Rivers. So they all came. Even the boys wanted to meet Sean, that's how popular he is.

Talitha, Hannah, Dakshima and I were easy to sort out. Adele on the other hand didn't want to go anywhere near Lycra. That was until Anne-Marie found her just the right top to wear, a looser, grey off-the-shoulder number with a pink trim, and let her off from having to wear the colour co-ordinated headband.

The boys on the other hand were immovable for quite some time.

"I ain't wearing no tights," Gabe said, looking in horror at some of the outfits that belonged to Anne-Marie's brother.

"You don't have to wear tights, man," Sean chuckled. "Just some sweats and a T-shirt, that's all – and maybe a headband and some legwarmers to protect your calves. Male dancers have to be really, really fit. Strong enough to lift a girl over their head and spin her round about a hundred times. None of this gear is for wimps."

Once Sean had talked Gabe into a pair of legwarmers and a vest, Gurkay, Rohan and the others all followed him.

"You look cute, Gabe," Talitha said, which made Gabe blush and Dakshima seethe, because she'd never have the guts to tell a boy he looked cute no matter how tough she might act.

When we were all finally kitted out, the twelve of us

stood in front of Anne-Marie's mirrored wardrobe doors and looked at our reflections.

"Mr Petrelli is going to do his nut," Rohan said.

"Or he'll be impressed with out initiative," I suggested.

"Maybe we'd better take our school uniforms too, just in case," Talitha said.

"Well, it's up to you," Anne Marie said, standing behind us with her arms crossed. "But at least you *look* like a chorus line. All you have to do now is try to sound like one."

Chapter Eight

"So," Dad said to me as we sat on the tube train on the way to the competition. "I never thought I'd be taking you to another audition so soon."

"It's not an audition," I said. "It's a competition. I haven't changed my mind. I want the school choir to do well. They've – *we've* – all really tried hard."

"And you've been a big help to them, I bet," Dad said. "What with all your professional training."

"Not really," I told him. "Although it is fun getting them to all act and move around the stage like a chorus. Plus Mr Petrelli is a good singing teacher. We sound pretty good now. Even I can carry a tune if I try hard. I've enjoyed being part of a group – a team."

"A pretty wacky team," Dad said, referring to the ankle-length raincoat I'd borrowed from Mum. Anne-Marie, me and Nydia were both adamant that the whole choir should turn up in our costumes, and pack their uniforms in case of a Mr Petrelli meltdown. But the rest of the choir weren't coming on the tube. I could have got a lift with someone else but I wanted to go with Dad.

"What do you think about Mum's news?" I asked him after a while.

"What news?" Dad said, seemingly studying a tube map very carefully.

"About Jeremy moving to London," I blurted out, making a few people look at me. "She did tell you, didn't she? Because if you've only just found out now then I'm sorry."

Dad sort of smiled and shook his head. "She told me," he said. "I'm fine about it. I'm happy for your mum that things are working out."

"Are you sure?" I asked. "Because even though I really like Jeremy, I want you to know that he'll never replace you, because you are my dad and I love you more than anything."

Dad put his arm around me. "Even though I know that, it's good to hear you say it, Ruby."

"Good," I said. "Just don't tell anyone that I did, OK?"

Dad smiled. "Anyway, I think I should be asking you how you feel about it," he said. "After all, I'm the parent here, right?"

"Right. But I already know how I feel about it," I said. "Because I'm me. And even though it's weird that just a year ago you and Mum and me were all living together and now things couldn't be more different, I'm fine about it. I'm getting used to everything changing all of the time. I don't think anything could surprise me any more."

"That's sort of how I feel too," Dad said after a moment.

"Really?" I asked.

"Ruby, your mum was really hurt and sad when we split up and I still care about her a lot. So knowing she's happy makes me happy for her. And if you like Jeremy then I like Jeremy."

"And what about you?" I asked him. "Are you still with your so-called girlfriend?"

"I thought we'd agreed we weren't going to call her that," Dad said, repressing a smile.

"We did, but it's funny and I thought as long as I said it with respect it would be OK," I said.

"Yes, I'm still with her," Dad said, stretching his legs out across the tube carriage. "Now, we're getting off at the next stop. Are you ready for the competition?"

I swallowed the butterflies that were trying hard to escape from my tummy. "Ready as I'll ever be." I said, as I tried to focus on what was about to happen.

Me, Ruby Parker, singing out loud in front of people.

What was the world coming to?

* * *

"Get your coats off," Mr Petrelli said as we all stood around in the side room we'd been allocated for our final rehearsal. "We only have half an hour to warm up before we have to compete."

Nobody moved.

"What's up – nerves?" Mr Petrelli asked anxiously. "Because I promise you you'll start to feel better once we start rehearsing. Now, take your places while I talk to the pianist."

Mr Petrelli turned his back on us and one by one we all took our coats off and moved into our rows.

When he turned back and saw us his jaw dropped.

For a long moment nobody said anything or even moved.

This is my fault, I thought. *It's me who'll have to say something.*

"We thought that maybe if we dressed in the style of the show it would help us stand out," I blurted. "But it was a silly idea, my friend's idea, my fault entirely. We all brought our uniforms to change back into, didn't we?"

Everyone nodded and murmured yes.

Mr Petrelli stood there, stock still, for a couple of seconds longer. Then, "Genius idea," he said slowly. "A totally genius idea! Yes, it's a bit off the wall and maybe the judges will hate it, but it's bold and decisive and I like it. Ruby, I've just promoted you to creative director!"

"What? Who, me?" I asked. "What does that mean?"

"It means that you're the one who's choreographed and styled us, and I don't think we would have had the confidence to get this far if it wasn't for you."

I glanced around as the others murmured agreement and clapped me on the back.

"Right, well," I said, suddenly feeling like I was really among friends. "In that case, let's knock 'em dead!"

"Cool," Gabe said, producing his headband from his pocket and jamming it on with a grin.

"I can't believe that's it," Dakshima said as we sat down in the holding room – a great big hall where all the competing choirs had to wait for the results. "All that build up and it was over in minutes."

"I know," Talitha said. "We remembered to do everything we were supposed to though, didn't we? We didn't make any mistakes, right?"

"Except that pianist played 'Alone in a Crowd' differently from Mr Petrelli," Adele said. "He played it faster. I think we were a bit late coming in on the final chorus."

"And what do you think the judges thought?" Gabe

said. "I think they thought we were losers."

"They look at everyone that way," Hannah said. "It's their job to try and scare us into being rubbish. It's so they know that we can take the pressure of a live performance."

"That *was* a live performance, even if it did nearly kill me," Gurkay said, smiling at me. "You did your solo better than you've ever done it before, Ruby."

"Really?" I said uncertainly. "I don't know. But the rest of you were really good. I think we did really, really well and we should be proud of ourselves whatever. When they give us the results we'll know we've tried our hardest and that's what counts."

"It'd be much better if we won though," Dakshima said.

"Totally," Gabe said.

Suddenly Mr Petrelli walked into the room, running his fingers through his hair.

"Hear anything, sir?" I asked.

He shook his head. "No, the judges are having a problem making their minds up. It's going to be at least another hour yet. Your parents are waiting in the auditorium, but you'll have to stay here I'm afraid. They don't want people wandering around because a TV crew are filming the auditions for the lead parts on the next floor up. They're going to bring in some drinks and snacks in a few minutes, so just sit tight here and I'll be back as soon as hear any more."

"I'm bored," Dakshima said, about two seconds later. "What shall we do?"

"I-spy?" I suggested.

"No, idiot, something better than that. Let's go and find Nydia an Anne-Marie, see if they've auditioned yet."

"We can't do that," I said. "We're not allowed. You heard what Mr Petrelli said – we have to sit here and wait, we're not supposed to mix with that lot."

"Honestly, Ruby Parker," Dakshima said. "You must be a good actress because you're not at all like Polly Harris in *The Lost Treasure of King Arthur*. You are really, *really* bad at rebelling,"

"Tell me something I don't know," I said.

"We'll be away for five minutes tops," Dakshima tried to persuade me. "We'll just have a look around. No one will even notice us."

"Um, we're dressed like the Kids from Fame," I reminded her.

"Yeah, and so are all of your stage school friends," Dakshima said. "We'll blend right in. Come on, please – I'm *bored*."

I wavered; it would be nice to see how Nydia and

Anne-Marie had got on. Find out if they'd already auditioned and wish them luck if they hadn't. "What about the others," I said under my breath.

"We'll tell them we're going to the loo," Dakshima whispered, before saying out loud. "We're going to the loo. Back in five."

I got up and followed her out into the corridor before I could change my mind.

"I'm afraid you have to stay in the holding room, girls." A security guard who was standing outside the door stopped us as we tried to walk casually past him.

"We are, but we need the loo," Dakshima told him. "You don't want us to wet ourselves do you?"

"Straight there and back then," the man said, as Dakshima dragged me in the opposite direction to the ladies' loo, at just at the exact moment a rather pretty blonde lady walked by and distracted him.

"That was so close," I whispered as we made it round the corner to the stairwell.

"*That* wasn't close," Dakshima said. "*This* is going to be close. You heard Mr Petrelli – we have to go upstairs to the next floor. That's where they're taping the auditions. *That* is where the fun begins."

We could hear the singing long before we found the conference room where they were holding the auditions.

There was a long line of chairs outside the room and ten or so people sitting on them, waiting in nervous silence to go in. None of them were Nydia or Anne-Marie.

"How can we get inside?" Dakshima said. "Maybe there's another door. Come on, act natural."

I was still wondering how to act natural while dressed in a pink leotard, dance tights and legwarmers as I followed her along the corridors. Eventually we began to hear the singing again and we realised that we had found our way to the other side of the room, the side that was sort of backstage. Another door that led into the same room was propped ajar by some filming equipment and a thick black power cable that disappeared down the corridor. There was a red light rigged up and a sign hanging off of the door handle that said FILMING IN PROGRESS DO NOT ENTER. But there didn't seem to be anyone on guard and if we could just get close enough, we'd be able to see inside the room.

"Let's go and look," Dakshima whispered.

"We are going to get caught," I hissed, feeling worried. "Bound to."

"Probably," Dakshima said, her eyes sparking. "But not definitely. Come on, Rubes. We'll just have a peep and then go back. I've always wanted to see what Mick Caruso looks like in real life. Like a bit of old bark if his photos are anything to go by."

"Well, I saw him at the Academy's open day last year and that's exactly what he looked like, so can we just go please?"

Dakshima glanced sideways at me, "Well I didn't see him at your artsy fartsy do and I want to have a look now. Come *on*."

"Fine," I said, my voice tense. "Let's just get it over with." Holding my breath, we crept closer to the crack in the door, stepping carefully over the equipment and cables.

The view into the room was restricted because there were at least ten crew in there; sound men, cameramen, a make-up lady, a director and a few others. We could just see the large yellow circle (the 'Spotlight') that had been placed on the floor for the singers to stand on, and the two judges – rock legend Mick Caruso and former West End leading lady Elaine Emerson.

"Next!" Mick Caruso shouted out.

I don't know how long we watched contestants come and go but once we started it was hard to stop. The longer we crouched with our eyes pressed to the crack in the door, the safer it felt.

Some of the auditionees were very good, and some of them were awful, but none got chosen to go through to the live televised final. A boy called Harry du Pont was so awful that Dakshima and I had to clap our hands over our mouths to stop ourselves from laughing out loud.

"Tell me I'm not that bad," I whispered in her ear, my shoulders shaking with suppressed mirth.

"You are no way that bad," Dakshima whispered back, her big brown eyes sparking. "Haven't you worked out that you're a pretty good singer yet, Ruby?"

"We'd better get back," I hissed. "We've been gone for ages."

Dakshima looked disappointed, but didn't protest. Then her eyes widened. "Wait! Look!"

I peered in through the crack. Danny was standing on the spotlight.

"We have to go," I said automatically, but neither of us moved.

"Well, Danny Harvey, we recognise you, of course," Mick said. "Tell us why you're auditioning for my new musical *Spotlight!*"

"Well, I love singing," Danny said. "I've always been a massive fan of yours, and of musicals..."

"Liar!" I exclaimed loud enough for Dakshima to dig me in the ribs. "He always said he thought musicals were for losers." I muttered sulkily.

"...And I really like lead character, Sebastian. He's wild

and rebellious, and I think I could play him really well."

"Well, you've got a head start," Mick Caruso said, leaning back in his chair and crossing his arms. "I don't think any of the other contestants here today have had a number one single. But your fame won't get you any special favours here, Danny. Not even my daughter is getting those. All we care about on the *Spotlight! Search for a Star* is true talent."

"I wouldn't want it any other way," Danny said, which sounded so unlike him that I was sure he was reciting a line he'd been given.

"Take it away, Danny," Elaine Emmerson said.

As Danny began to sing 'You Take Me To...', Dakshima and I looked at each other in total horror. The sound that was coming out of his mouth was nothing like his voice on the record. It was dreadful. I wished I could get a look at Danny's face, but we could only see him from the back. *He must be feeling dreadful*, I thought. *It's embarrassing.* Yet he carried on until he'd completed one chorus and another verse. I braced myself for the judge's comments.

"Amazing," Mick said. "What an incredible talent."

"It certainly was distinctive," Elaine Emmerson said uncertainly.

"You're going through the live final," Mick told him. "Congratulations, Danny."

"Er... thank you," Danny sounded uncertain. "I'm never really that sure I'm any good, but I suppose if people keep telling me I am..."

"You've got a great attitude," Mick said. "Good luck for the final."

Danny left the room and Dakshima and I looked at each other in astonishment.

"That was well rank," Dakshima said.

"He was pants," I said, nearly forgetting to whisper.

"Can we have a tea break before we have to subject our eardrums to any more?" we heard Mick call out. "Milk and two sugars, please, Lucy."

"Well, we've put him through," Elaine said. "I have to say, Mick, I don't approve of this at all."

"I know, I know," Mick said. "But if it makes Jade happy then it's worth it. She wants Danny Harvey as her leading man so it's Danny she is going to get."

"He's a great actor," Elaine said. "It's just a shame that he can't sing at all – even with his charm and good looks I don't know how you are going to cover that up and still look credible. This is live television, Mick. Not a recording studio where you can make anyone sound good. Miming won't cut it."

"I know that," Mick said. "But we'll get it sorted."

"I know better than most people that Carmen Baptista

is a genius when it comes to choreographing and staging a musical, but do you seriously think that she can teach Danny and Jade to sing like stars in less than a month?" Elaine asked.

"She won't have to," Mick said, lowering his voice. Dakshima and I leant nearer to the door. "Not once we've got them wired up to an Auto-tune Miracle Microphone."

Elaine didn't say anything, but I assume she must have looked puzzled because Mick Caruso explained. "It's a tiny device fitted inside a microphone just like the one musical actors wear on stage. The only difference is that whatever the actor sings into it is instantly retuned to sound fantastic in a fraction of a second, and then feeds through the speakers as live. No matter how bad the singing, the Auto-tune Miracle Microphone can make it sound brilliant. And the best thing is that the audience in the studio and at home will never know the difference." Mick chuckled. "It's going to make my Jade and that Danny the hottest two musical stars in the country."

There was a long pause.

"I don't like this at all," Elaine said uncertainly. "Mick, I don't want to be involved in something that means cheating the public and those kids."

"No one is getting cheated if everyone is happy," Mick

said. "Plenty of kids will get a chance to let their talent shine, but Jade and Danny need a little bit of extra help. And because I'm Jade's dad, I'm going to make sure she gets it. Nobody will ever know."

"If this gets out," Elaine said, "the reputation I've worked hard for will be shot to pieces. I don't think I can go on with this, Mick."

"I think you can, Elaine," Mick said. "For one thing, if you check your contract you'll find that you're stitched up tighter than a kipper. So think about those kids you *can* help and stop worrying about Jade."

"Hey, you!"

Dakshima and I fell over each other as we heard someone shout behind us.

"*Run!*" Dakshima yelled, grabbing my hand and racing down the corridor.

"Come back here!" the security guard yelled as we pelted around the corner and away.

"Stairs!" Dakshima breathed hard as she yanked at my arm. "Come *on*, Ruby!"

We scrambled down one flight of stairs and tumbled into the corridor on the floor where our holding room was.

"Here," Dakshima took her scrunchie out and handed it to me, shaking her long hair over her shoulders. "Put you hair up in this and give me your headband. Act natural, OK?"

"OK," I said squeakily, twisting my hair into a bun.

We strolled back into the holding room full of students, about five seconds before the security guard burst in. He stood stock still breathing heavily, looking around the room.

"Any one just run in here?" he asked. A room full of nervous kids stared blankly at him. "Right, well, if you see anyone running, let me know. We've had a serious breach of security."

Dakshima and I looked at each other as we sat down with the rest of the choir.

"Where have you two been?" Mr Petrelli said. "They're going to announce who's going through to the finals any minute now."

"We went to the loo," Dakshima said, looking at me. "We were nervous, weren't we, Ruby?"

"Very, very nervous," I said. I still couldn't believe what we'd overheard. I couldn't believe that anyone – not even Jade Caruso's dad – would give the lead parts in his musical to two kids who couldn't sing. I couldn't believe that he was *cheating* so much. I could only hope that Jade wouldn't have any say about anyone else, which meant that Anne-Marie and Nydia still had a good chance of getting one of the lead roles.

It seemed to take a long time before Highgate Comprehensive School Choir was called through to hear our fate. Other choirs went out one by one, but as they didn't come back in again, we still had no idea what was happening. Finally there were just two choirs left – ours and St Mildred's School for Girls, a very good choir all dressed immaculately in tartan kilts and blazers. Suddenly I felt a bit silly in my legwarmers.

The door swung open.

"Right, can the last two choirs come through to the auditorium, please," the blonde production assistant said.

We all stood in a row in front of the judges. This time there were TV cameras, and Mick Caruso and Elaine Emmerson had joined the judging panel.

"Hello, choirs," Lillian Shoreditch, the head judge, began to speak. "You were the best two choirs in the competition today…"

There were cheers from both choirs and looks of stunned disbelief from a few of the Highgate Comp kids, not to mention Mr Petrelli.

"You each had different strengths. St Mildred's, your performances were a technical tour de force, the sounds you made utterly beautiful – and you must be commended for being the only choir here today to achieve such a high standard of singing."

A ripple of applause momentarily broke the tension in the auditorium.

"Highgate Comprehensive – you brought something completely fresh and original to the competition, with your very successful attempts at staging the songs and your unique approach to costume. You gave us some much need showbusiness and reminded us that we are looking for a West End chorus and not a school choir."

Lillian Shoreditch picked up a piece of paper. "It's been a very tough decision, but the choir going through the national final of the competition is…"

And we waited…

And we waited…

And just when I couldn't stand it any longer she read out, "Highgate Comprehensive School Choir – you've won!"

And suddenly I was engulfed in hugs and my ears

were filled with shouts and screams and all I could think was... "We've got through to the final. We did it!"

One thing I knew for sure though was that our choir had got through because we'd tried really hard and did the best we could. Nobody rigged our result, not like Danny's.

The question was, now that I knew about Danny, Jade and the Auto-tune Miracle Microphone, what was I going to do about it?

Saturday 25th Top Choice! **Star Pick of the day!**

SPOTLIGHT!: SEARCH FOR A STAR THE FINAL **7.05 p.m.**

There's really only one show worth watching this Saturday and it's **SPOTLIGHT!: SEARCH FOR A STAR THE FINAL**. We've all been waiting with baited breath since iconic rocker Mick Caruso announced that he was planning to turn his pantheon of classic hits into a musical that was to star only under-sixteens and premiere with a live performance on TV. Mick's own daughter Jade Caruso has gone through rigorous auditions to win her place in this live final and we'll see some other more familiar faces competing alongside unknown talent too. Danny Harvey of **Kensington Heights** fame will be hoping for your phone vote, as well as popular children's TV presenter Nydia Assimin. Also look out for the face of H&M summer teen collection Anne-Marie Chance. All four of these hopefuls are pupils of the legendary Sylvia Lighthouse Academy for the Performing Arts. Cue tears, tantrums, hopes and dreams dashed, and much, much more! Can there be a better way to spend your Saturday night? RF

(NB: Look out for the finalist of the choir competition; our old favourite Ruby Parker is making a low key appearance in one of the choirs hoping the win a place in the chorus and £20,000 for their school. Everyone here at *Top Choice!* misses young Ruby and we hope this is the start of a comeback.)

Chapter Nine

"It *is* kind of amazing that *all* of your friends got a place in the final," Dakshima said, as she read the piece in the TV guide out on our way to our last rehearsal before the national final. "*Maybe* their results were rigged too. *Maybe* ours were. Maybe we only got picked for the national choirs final because of *you*!"

It had been two weeks since we found out that we were going through the final. Two weeks of solid rehearsing in which we found out that Anne-Marie and Nydia were going to join Jade and Danny in the final for the lead parts too. And two weeks since Dakshima and I found out that Danny had got through, not because of his talent, but because Jade had wanted him to. Mick Caruso had been rigging the results.

So far Dakshima and I hadn't told anyone. We didn't know who to tell or even if we should.

"They didn't put our choir through because of me," I told her, shaking my head. "Jade hates me so much that we'd have been out in the first five minutes if she'd had a say in it. They put us through because we were the most original, so forget about worrying that we don't deserve it. And I *know* that Nydia is one of the best singers I've ever heard and that Anne-Marie can belt out a show tune like a star. Those two deserve to have a chance. Besides, you heard Mick Caruso; he told Elaine that it was only Danny and Jade that he was going to plug into that microphone thingy, everyone else would be there on their merits."

"I suppose so," Dakshima said. "But it's just not right that those two should get the places that two other kids really deserve."

"Well, they might not," I said slowly. "I mean, there's the phone vote. Maybe people won't vote for them.

Dakshima looked at me. "Do you really think that Mick's going to let that happen to his little girl? Either the show will make them look so good people vote for them, or they'll rig the results – you hear about it all the time. Either way, they'll get through, I'm telling you."

"What should we do?" I asked her.

"What do you mean, what should we do?" she replied.

"Well, we know this thing and it's a really terrible and wrong thing – shouldn't we tell someone? Maybe Mr Petrelli?"

Dakshima frowned. "I don't know," she said. "I mean

maybe this is what it's like. Maybe this is the real reality of reality TV. Besides, if we tell someone now then the show might be stopped completely and we wouldn't get a chance to be in it and the school won't get the prize money. And there are more people who do deserve to be in *Spotlight!* than the two who don't. I think we should forget what we heard, keep our heads down and hope our choir wins."

"It's just..." I paused, feeling uneasy. "I'm sure if Danny knew that he was being manipulated like this he'd be really upset and he wouldn't have anything to do with it. I know he dumped me for Melody in a letter, and at the worst time of my life, but he'd hate to think he got through because of cheating. And he wouldn't want the part just because the producer's daughter fancies him. He's not *that* bad."

"Are you sure he's not like that?" Dakshima asked me, hooking her arm through mine. "You said he told you he hated musicals, and then we saw him in front of the cameras going on about how much he loved them. Maybe he knows what Mick is planning for him."

I shook my head. "No, not Danny. He's a stubborn idiotic pig, but he's not evil."

Dakshima laughed. "You are *so* not over him," she said, ducking as I swiped at her with my bag.

Dakshima was right though; Danny had said he loved musicals at the audition, something I didn't think he would ever normally say, even to get a part. The truth was that the Danny I knew and the Danny that was going to be singing live on national TV in a couple of days' time seemed like a completely different person. Plus Anne-Marie and Nydia said he hadn't been hanging out with them since the auditions, so I couldn't even ask them what they thought.

"Is he hanging around with Jade?" I'd asked Anne-Marie on the phone last night, trying and failing to sound casual.

"No, he's trying to escape from her I think," Anne-Marie had said. "She's all over him like a rash. I don't know why he's cooled it with us, though. He's not even hanging about with Sean any more. Maybe it's because Melody didn't get through and he doesn't want to rub her nose in the fact that the rest of us breezed it."

I'd found myself wondering if Melody not getting through had something to do with Jade's plans for Danny.

"Look, if you think Danny would hate what's happening, then it's obvious what you should do," Dakshima said, as we walked to the music room. "Why don't you tell him?"

"*Tell* him?" I asked her, stupidly surprised by the suggestion.

"Yes, go and see him and tell him what you overheard. I mean, he's not an idiot is he? He must be able to work out that the sound he's hearing in his head is completely different to the one coming out of the speakers?"

"I don't know," I said uncertainly, lowering my voice to a whisper. "Don't you think that would be a bit weird? For me, his ex-girlfriend, to go and tell him that his whole singing career is a fake?"

Dakshima shrugged. "Well, you said he'd hate it if he knew the truth. If you tell him, then he'll know. He can make the right choice for him, instead of being pushed around by that Jade and her family without even realising it. As long as we still get our chance to be in the chorus and win the money for the school. I'm not saying blow the whole thing wide open, I'm saying give him a chance to back out before it's too late."

"You're right," I said, feeling more nervous about talking to Danny than I did singing solo. "I have to tell him. There's only one problem."

"What's that?" Dakshima asked me as we filed into the class.

"If I tell him that means I'll actually have to talk to him," I said. "And I'm not entirely sure I can do that."

Standing outside Danny's house later that day, I looked up at his bedroom window. The curtains were drawn and the light was on, so he was in.

I suppose I could have phoned or texted him first, but I didn't want him to know that I still had his number programmed into my phone, and that anyway, even if I didn't, I knew it off by heart. Besides, I got the feeling that if he knew I was coming then he wouldn't be in – after all, why would he want to see me?

Still, now I was here, the thought of knocking on the door and going through with it, never mind actually having to talk to him with actual words, made me feel queasy. He could be in there with Melody, or even Jade. He could be plotting his next evil master plan to conquer to the world of musicals despite his total lack of singing talent at that very moment... and then I stopped.

This was Danny, I reminded myself. He always stood up for what he believed in, even when he was completely wrong. That was one of the best and most annoying things about him. I rang the doorbell and had to glue my feet to the step to stop myself from running away in the twenty or so seconds it took for someone to come and open the door.

Danny's mum appeared, her tense expression melting when she saw it was me.

"Hello, Ruby," she said, her voice warm and friendly. "We haven't seen you in such a long time. Come on in. Danny's upstairs going over his audition piece again and I'm sure he'd appreciate a break from all that noise… singing, I mean, and an expert opinion like yours." She lowered her voice. "I must be tone deaf, Ruby. I can't hear what everyone else can when he's practising here at home. But don't tell him I said that, OK? He's nervous enough as it is."

I nodded and stood at the bottom of the stairs, looking up at them as if at the top was a very high precipice I was about to throw myself off.

"Well, go up then," Danny's mum prompted me, wincing as Danny missed a particularly high note.

Desperately wishing that I hadn't come round at all and wondering what had ever possessed me to have such a bad idea, I started heavily up the stairs. It was the longest walk of my life, longer than any red carpet or corridor leading to an audition. After briefly considering climbing out through the bathroom window and shinning down a drainpipe, I took a breath, steeled myself, knocked on his door and waited.

"Come in," Danny said. And when I appeared, he dropped the sheet music he was holding. "Oh, Ruby! Ruby – um, hi, hello... I didn't expect to see you."

"I can go..." I began backing away.

"No, no, don't. Not if you don't want to... either way – whatever," Danny said, and then, "Come in and sit down."

I sat down at his paper strewn desk and swivelled the chair to look at him.

The trouble with Danny was that he was still really cute. If the world was a fair place, the moment he dumped me he should have grown enormous ears, had all his hair fall out and got terrible acne. But he didn't. He was just as fit as he had been when I first realised I liked him. The world, I knew now, was not a fair place.

"So," Danny said stiffly. "How can I help you?"

"Help me?" I asked him. "You make it sound like I've come to buy a pair of shoes or something."

"Did I?" Danny said. "I didn't mean to. I just didn't expect to see you. Like you and I were still friends. I mean, are we?"

"I... I don't know, Danny," I said. "I've never tried being friends with an ex-boyfriend before."

Danny gave me a hint of a smile that made my heart

feel as if someone was squeezing it really hard. "I'd really like to have you around again, Ruby," he said. I was silent for what seemed like forever until Danny added, "As a friend, of course."

"OK, well..." I had no idea how to steer the conversation around to what I wanted to tell him and now he had brought up the whole "liking me as a friend thing" it seemed even harder.

"Are you nervous about Saturday?" I asked. "Singing live in front of millions of people must be scary. Then again, I suppose you've done it before so you'll be fine."

"I haven't actually *sung* live on TV before," Danny said, looking worried. "When I did live performances of 'You Take Me To...' I always mimed along to the recording. I *am* nervous about it. Mum says when I practise my song here that my voice doesn't sound anything like it does on the recording and I agree with her. In my head it sounds terrible. But I went to the dress rehearsal last night and they wired me up to the mike and I sounded completely different, really good. I guess that what I hear in my head isn't what everyone else hears – do you find that?"

"Um," I said. "Look, Danny, the thing is—"

"Ruby," Danny interrupted me, "I know what you're going to say..."

"You do?" I asked. "When? How did you find out?"

"Well, you coming round made it pretty obvious," Danny said. "The thing is, I don't know if now it's the right time. I mean, I've got the live final coming up and Melody is already really upset about not getting through. I do feel the same way, but maybe we should wait a while."

I blinked at him. "Wait - *what's* obvious?"

"You want to go out with me again," Danny said, smiling and taking my hand.

"*What?* You thought I came round here for *that*?" I said, standing up and snatching my hand back, swooshing a few of his papers to the floor.

"Well, didn't you?" Danny asked me, frowning deeply.

"No I did not!" I yelled at him. "Honestly, Danny Harvey, since you started on *Kensington Heights* and had a Christmas number one, you think the world revolves around you!"

"Really?" Danny said, waving his rolled up sheet music at me. "And what about you? You think you are the centre of the universe—"

"I don't!" I protested.

"Disappear off to Hollywood, start up a career, and when that all goes wrong, stick your head in the sand and expect us all to feel sorry for you while you pretend you aren't who you are. You said you wanted to give up acting, Ruby, but dropping out of the Academy has to be one of the most drama queen things you've *ever* done!"

"You... I... *grrrrrrr*."

Yes, I actually growled at Danny Harvey. I was so furious with him for being so right and so wrong about me at exactly the same time.

"I don't know why I even bother, Danny!" I shouted at him. "You make a fool of yourself in front of eight million people. I don't care, and you know what else?"

"What?" Danny said crossing his arms.

"I'd rather nail my hand to the floor than go out with you again," I told him.

"Good," he said.

"Good," I said.

And then I ran down the stairs and out of the front door as fast as I could.

"Not staying for tea, Ruby?" I heard his mum call out after me as I fled.

"Love Gets it Wrong
Every Time"

Words and music by *Mick Caruso*

I've had my heart broken a hundred times
Trampled by a thousand cruel crimes
But when I saw you I thought my luck had finally changed
You smiled at me and my life rearranged

I thought you were the one who would finally be mine!
But now I know…
Love gets it wrong every time.

Love gets it wrong!
I made a mistake when I trusted you with my heart
Love gets it wrong!
I should have known that you lied from the start!
Love gets it wrong!
But now I understand that you'll never be mine
Because love gets it wrong every time.

You lured me in with your smile
Planning how you'd hurt me all the while
I really believed every single word that you said

But you lied, and now I can't get you out of my head.

I was so wrong when I thought that you would be mine
Because now I know…
Love gets it wrong every time.

Love gets it wrong!
I made a mistake when I trusted you with my heart
Love gets it wrong!
I should have known that you lied from the start!
Love gets it wrong!
But now I understand that you'll never be mine
Because love gets it wrong every time.

Chapter Ten

"He said *what*?" Dakshima asked me as we climbed into the minibus that was taking us to the studio for the choir competition finals.

"That he thought I went round there to ask him back out," I exclaimed still outraged.

"And did you?"

"No, I did not…" I replied with some consternation, before glancing over my shoulder and lowering my voice. "You *know* why I went round there."

"Oh, OK," Dakshima said. "I just thought that might have been cover for you wanting to ask him back out."

"It was your idea for me to go round!" I exclaimed loudly enough to make Mr Petrelli look at me.

"Focus please, Ruby," he said. "Today is one of the most important days of our lives. It's up to us to use the hard work we've put in to the best possible advantage and show the judges that we've got what they are looking for. It will be an incredible achievement if we beat all the other choirs to become part of the chorus on

Spotlight! but I really think we can do it. We've already shown them that we are more than a choir, we're performers!" We all whooped and cheered. "So let's go and show them what we can do!" Mr Petrelli shouted quite loudly.

"OK!" we all yelled in response, clapping and cheering as the minibus pulled out of the school car park. I waved at Mum and Dad who had decided to go to the competition together and were going to meet me at the TV studios.

"So, what did he say?" Dakshima asked me, as we turned the corner on to the High Road.

"Who?" I asked her, chewing my thumbnail and thinking about my solo.

"Danny. What did Danny say?" Dakshima asked me.

"I told you," I said with exasperation. "He thought I'd gone round to get back with him—"

"*No*, what did he say when you told him about the Auto-tune Miracle thingummy," Dakshima interrupted me before I could tell her the whole story again.

"Oh, I... sort of... didn't *exactly* tell him," I said staring nonchalantly out of the window.

"You didn't *tell* him?" Dakshima repeated, looking far more surprised than I thought was appropriate.

"Well, I got so mad," I explained. "I was so mad that

I actually growled like an angry dog, and I thought, well, fine, if he thinks he is so great, then what can I do to change that? Nothing, so why tell him?"

"Okey-*dokey*," Dakshima said slowly. "Well... I guess it's too late now."

"Yes, it is," I said, desperate to justify what I'd done, or rather hadn't done. "And anyway, he's better off not knowing. He'll go on stage tonight and everyone will think he's wonderful and he'll get the lead in the show and he'll be happy. Deluded, but happy, and why should I even care?"

"Unless..." Dakshima said.

"Unless what?"

"Sometimes equipment has a habit of going wrong," she said menacingly.

"Dakshima! You wouldn't sabotage Danny's microphone, would you?" I asked, scandalised. "I mean, I know he's a pig and everything, but if something happened while he was singing in front of all of those people, that would just be awful. I'd *never* do that to him!"

"Of course I wouldn't," Dakshima said. "I am not an *evil* genius. Anyway, I only said that to check how you reacted and it's exactly as I thought – you are *so* not over Danny Harvey."

"I so *am*," I protested. "And anyway, what's done is done. Now is the time to focus on today. We'll forget about the microphone, Danny and Jade and everything. All we should think about is giving the best performance we possibly can."

"And winning," Dakshima added.

"And maybe even winning," I agreed, feeling the nerves bunching in my tummy. "Just maybe."

There were eight choirs in the competition final, which was going to be filmed in the TV studio next door to where the live TV show would be broadcast later on in the day. The choir competition was to be cut and edited into the main show later. That meant that the studio lights were bright and hot and there were TV cameras everywhere.

As I felt the warmth of the lights on my face I realised what was different between me and the other kids from Highgate Comprehensive. Here in the TV studio I felt at home, with the lights, the equipment, crew and even the smell. More than that, I hadn't realised how much I missed the sense of anticipation that something exciting was about to happen.

The others behaved very differently. The boys, led by

Gabe and Rohan, started acting the fool in front of the unmanned cameras, and a few of the girls – Adele in particular – were frightened of the whole set up. It was the cameras that freaked them out, and the thought of being on the other end of what they usually saw beamed into their the sitting rooms at home.

"Just try to ignore them," I told Adele as she stared at one that was right in front of the stage we'd be singing on.

"How can I ignore that?" Adele asked. "It's massive and it's looking right at me with one evil eye."

"It's just a machine," I said. "And behind it is just the cameraman, the director, the editor – that's all."

"That many?" Adele asked me, wide eyed.

"That's a lot less than we sang in front of in the first round," I said. "Come on, Adele, just think of them all as a bit of equipment, nothing more."

"I suppose," Adele said uncertainly.

"That's the spirit," I said, clapping her on the back.

I looked around at the studio. There were school choirs from Scotland, Wales, Northern Ireland, the South West, the South East, the Midlands, the North and us. We were the London choir.

The choir from Northern Ireland had had the same costume idea as ours, except theirs all matched. I thought our variations were more authentic. Plus, since we won the London heat, we'd been working on a few more dance steps to make us seem even more like a proper chorus. Nydia and Anne-Marie, who were real dancers, had helped us with that. Since we got through the heat I really started to believe that we actually could win the place in the chorus line of the show and I'd even let myself start to be excited by the thought. It would be perfect, because I'd be there, on stage and in a show, part of something that I love so much and yet nobody would be looking especially at me. Nobody would notice if I got it wrong or if I wasn't good enough. No one would be able to judge me like they had done so cruelly in Hollywood.

"This is what's going to happen," the director, Sam Taylor, told all of us. "We'll be running the competition as live and filming all of it. That means no stopping, no second takes or second chances. You all have to do your best the first time, OK? You will perform your songs in the allocated order, the judges will comment and then you'll be moved into the holding area to await the results. Any questions?"

Adele's hand hovered hesitantly in the air.

"Yes?"

"Can I go to the toilet, please?"

* * *

Click… click… click, five, six, seven, eight and reach, and reach. I wasn't thinking about anything else except for the steps that we had worked out to go with 'Alone in a Crowd.' Step and step and step and pivot.

I assumed my position at the front right-hand of the stage area while I waited for Talitha, Hannah and Dakshima to sing their parts. Talitha went first, and then took one, two, three steps, touching Hannah on the arm. Hannah started to sing and then came forward and tapped Dakshima on the arm.

Dakshima did not move.

There was a split second when everything nearly went horribly wrong. I looked at Dakshima and I realised that despite all of her tough talking and confidence, she was caught in the glare of the spotlight and somehow it had frozen her solid.

Oh no, I began to think, but before I could even frame the words in my mind I heard another voice singing. Adele walked forward into Dakshima's light like she was born to be the centre of attention, and put all the power and passion she had into the lines that were supposed to be Dakshima's. And as she sang, she put her arm around Dakshima, breaking the spell of the spotlight, and the two of them sang together as they walked over to me. Only seconds had passed and yet I had felt I had been on a rollercoaster ride, my heart was beating so hard – and now it was my turn to sing solo.

Well, after that I knew I couldn't let them down.

And then suddenly it was over. The performance that would either win the school the prize and get us into the show, or send us home tonight, was finished and there was nothing else we could do to change it now.

I was surprised by how much I cared about what happened next, because if I was honest it wasn't just the choir and the school I wanted to win it for, it was for *me* too. I wanted to be a part of my dream again. Even if it was just a very little and unimportant part. I knew it would fill the gap that had been there ever since I had given up acting. Even if it was only for a while.

"You were so good," my mum said, coming over and hugging me.

"You were all fantastic," Dad said, giving the rest of the choir a thumbs-up.

"I wasn't," Dakshima said flatly. "I nearly ruined it for all of us. I don't know what happened. I was ready and confident, and then my moment came and nothing happened. I forgot the words, the steps, the tune. I forgot what my name was for a second!"

"That happens sometimes," I said, patting her on the back. "It's called freezing, and the only thing you can do about it is to cover it – and that's exactly what we did because Adele saved the day!"

The rest of the choir all cheered Adele who blushed like a berry.

"You were amazing, all of you," Mr Petrelli said. "But Adele, you are my hero. When we get back to school I'll be recommending you for a commendation."

"Me?" Adele said in surprise, smiling and waving at her mum, who was coming across the room with Dakshima's parents. "I've never had one of them."

"You deserve it," I said. "I'm glad you threatened me on my first day at Highgate Comp, otherwise you and I might not have been friends now."

"I'm glad I threatened you too," Adele said, before rushing off to hug her mum.

"It's odd," I said to Dakshima once her parents and brothers and sisters had stopped telling how proud they were of her. "The judges are off deciding who to choose, but I sort of feel like we've come so far that we've already won."

"That is so lame," Dakshima said. "Or is that a quote from *The Underdogs*?"

"OK, I might be soppy," I teased her, "but at least I didn't freeze on stage."

"Don't even talk about it!" Dakshima cringed. "If we don't win it's because of me."

"Don't be crazy," I said. "Remember what Sean actually *does* say in *The Underdogs*."

"*If a little person has a big enough heart, then anything is possible*," we chorused.

I expected some sort of heart pounding music. You know, the kind that *goes Dum... Dum... Dummm...* but as all eight choirs lined up for the results there was no music at all. I supposed they put it on afterwards. Instead there was near silence, peppered with nervous coughs and shuffling feet.

"Well," Simon Taylor said. "May I just say that you have all done yourselves proud today? Every single one of you has given it your best shot. Before we announce who the winners are, we need to tell you that the winning choirs will go straight from here to rehearsal and will be singing on tonight's live show with the winning leads."

There was a gasp and some chatter from the waiting choirs, because even though we had already known that, hearing someone say it out loud made it feel almost close enough to touch.

"But that's just the start," Simon Taylor told us. "If your choir is chosen to be part of the chorus of *Spotlight!* you will also win £20,000 for your school and go into rehearsal for next month's televised charity premiere performance of *Spotlight! The Musical.*"

I clapped and cheered along with everyone else.

"So with out further ado," Simon Taylor said, "let me hand over to your head judge, Miss Lillian Shoreditch!"

This time there was a ripple of nervous applause.

"This has been a very hard choice to make and on behalf of all the judges here I just want to say how impressed we are with all of the school choirs..."

"Yeah, yeah, whatever," Dakshima said under her breath, as Lillian Shoreditch went on about the bright future for the musical arts in the UK. "Just tell us who's won already!"

"But there can only be one winner," Lillian Shoreditch said. "And I am very pleased to announce that the winning choir, who won because of their obvious commitment and innovation, as well as their considerable talent, is Highgate Comprehensive!"

The noise that erupted all around me was so loud that for a moment I stood stock still, not really certain of what I had heard at all. We all stared at each other for a split second before leaping about and cheering ourselves.

"We did it!" Mr Petrelli yelled in a most unteacherly way. "We did it – *woohoo!*"

Chapter Eleven

We spent the next four hours on the set on the live show rehearsing our part, which was to accompany the finalists. But although we sang, the finalists didn't. They just came and stood on their marks and walked through their choreography.

Nydia waved at me like crazy when she saw me, now wearing black trousers and a black T-shirt with the *Spotlight!* logo on it like everyone else in the choir – now the chorus – had been given to wear for the show. When it was Anne-Marie's turn she ignored me completely, but I didn't take it personally. She had told me that morning that throughout the entire day she would be staying "in the zone", which meant that she would be thinking about nothing except for the performance she was going to give that night. Once she was in the zone, she explained, she'd be ignoring pretty much everyone until she had finished her song.

It took a while to calm us all down because we were so excited, but after four hours' hard rehearsal with the legendary choreographer and singing coach Carmen Baptista, a scarily strict lady, we soon settled down. Especially after she told us that competition winners or not, if we didn't come up to scratch she'd be booting our behinds out of the door faster than we could say "Spotlight".

"It feels a bit odd," Mr Petrelli said, when we took a break from rehearsal. "Handing you over to someone else to put you through your paces."

"We'll still need a ton of practice," Talitha said.

"Yeah, we're only allowed to rehearse twice a week," Gabe added. "I think we should still come to choir practice on Wednesday lunchtimes."

Mr Petrelli spent quite a long time trying not to look too pleased. "Well, I should think so too," he said eventually. "I expect nothing less of you."

Just before the show was due to go live, we were sat in a section of the audience, ready to file out and take our places when the finalists came out. There were twelve of them including Danny, Jade, Anne-Marie, Nydia – three more girls and five more boys. There were four lead roles in the show – Arial, Sebastian, Serena and Jake and as I knew that two of those had already been cast I wondered which of the others would win. I really hoped that at least one of my friends would get the other female lead

– but which one? And how would the one who got left out feel about not making it through? I was so confused about what I knew, it made my head hurt thinking about it. I just had to wait and see what happened. For now that was only thing that I could do.

Then the show's theme tune – a medley of songs from the show – was played in the studio and one of the production team gave the audience the signal to start cheering and clapping.

I found myself clutching on to Dakshima's hand, I was more nervous now than I had been when we were competing. I was nervous for Anne-Marie and Nydia – and especially Danny. What if something did go wrong? What if he was caught out on live TV as a cheat and I never did anything to prevent it, just because of that silly argument we'd had at his house?

"Lay off, Ruby, you're cutting off my circulation," Dakshima whispered, prising my fingers off of hers.

"Sorry," I said. "Nerves."

"It's not you who's got to be nervous though," Dakshima reminded me.

The presenter, Brianna McCloud, came on in a sparkly gold dress and waited for the applause to die down.

"Well, this is it," she told the TV audience at home as

she smiled into the camera lens like it was her best friend. "The moment we've all been waiting for, when we will find out who will be playing the leads in *Spotlight!* the new musical for young people. We've searched the country far and wide looking for the nation's best talent under the age of sixteen, and after seeing more than eleven thousand hopefuls, we've picked out twelve finalists for you to choose from. It wasn't an easy choice... here are just some of the stars of tomorrow that we met along the way."

The video package of auditions came up on a big screen in the studio and we watched as some of the best and worst people who'd tried out for the final were shown. Towards the end they flashed up a few seconds of Danny's audition, and Dakshima and I looked at each other. He didn't sound anything like he had on the actual day.

"Wonderful," Brianna said, looking up at the big screen before turning back to the camera and giving it a twinkly smile. "So now let me introduce you to our panel of judges. First, the creator of all of those wonderful songs we know so well, now featuring in his amazing new show *Spotlight!* – it's rock legend and musical genius, Mick Caruso!"

Brianna waited for the applause to finish. "And at Mick's side, as always, his best friend, successful theatre producer and recording breaking show impresario, Kevin Hillson!"

"Kevin Hillson isn't a very impresario type name, is it?" Dakshima whispered.

"Takes all sorts," I whispered back. "I wonder if he knows about the Auto-tune Miracle Microphone too?"

"Bound to," Dakshima said, before feeling heat from the glare that Carmen Baptista was sending our way. We pressed our lips together and looked straight ahead. We didn't want to get into trouble with Carmen.

"And finally, West End leading lady and worldwide recording star, Elaine Emmerson!"

Dakshima and I looked at each other but we didn't say a word. Carmen was still watching us.

It seemed to take an age for Brianna to go through her chat with the judges, and then we had to watch another video package of the first hopeful. While that was being screened, Carmen gave the signal and we all filed past her (Dakshima and I keeping our eyes down) and on to our spots at the back of the set.

The first finalist out was a girl from Stoke on Trent called Michaela Mathews and she was singing a song I had only learnt that afternoon, called 'Starlight Dreams'.

I sang along with the rest of the chorus as Michaela did her stuff, but I wasn't really listening. I was trying to work out how long it would be until Danny came on. The line up went girl, boy, girl, boy, and Jade and Danny were the last two on, probably because the producers would have to adjust the sound equipment to allow for their 'special' microphones.

The next boy, Callum Murphy, was really good and got loads of whoops and cheers from audience. Elaine Emmerson told him she could see him commanding the stage with no problem, despite the fact he was only fourteen.

And then it was Nydia.

This time she didn't smile and wave at me as she walked out to take her place. I could tell she was nervous because as she picked up the microphone there was a slight tremor in her hand. But as soon as she started singing 'Alone in a Crowd' she was wonderful. As she finished the last line, the audience stood up and the cheering seemed to go on for so long that Brianna had to stop everyone in case the show ran over time and made *Match of the Day* late.

Mick Caruso told Nydia that it lifted his heart to see such a versatile young actress. He hoped the audience at home would see it wasn't Nydia's TV profile that got her a place in the final, it was her amazing voice.

Hypocrite, I thought, as Nydia walked off beaming.

Another boy, David Rubenfeld, and then the next girl, Elizabeth Ashley, went on, and the more I waited for Danny's turn, the less real it seemed that I was standing in a TV studio that millions of people were viewing live. I tried to imagine being at home and watching me on TV, but it made my head hurt. Besides, as Danny's turn got nearer I began to feel a little queasy.

Looking amazing with her blonde curls bouncing and in a wonderful pair of jeans that glittered with sequins, Anne-Marie came on to sing. She'd been given 'Spotlight' and as it was the number that Mick Caruso was planning to release as a single, she knew she had to give it everything.

She was fantastic, moving around the stage, dancing as she sang with total confidence and flair, something that none of the other finalists had done, not even Nydia. Although Nyds had a stronger voice than Anne-Marie, she wasn't quite as much of a performer as my other best friend. Finally out of her zone, Anne-Marie grinned and winked at me as she walked off, and I knew she was pleased with how she'd done.

Just before Jade's turn there was a video package of the choir's competition. We all watched ourselves on the big screen as they showed clips of our audition, including Dakshima's stone cold terrified face as she realised she'd forgotten everything and Adele stepping in, which made the crowd laugh and then cheer, and Dakshima blush under Carmen Baptista's scrutiny.

Then Mick introduced Jade, telling everyone that although he'd offered her the lead role of Arial from the very start, and even though he'd really created the musical for her and to give young people like her a chance to shine, she had wanted to prove that she deserved the part and not have it handed to her on a plate like everyone would expect.

Jade came out and performed the simplest song for the show, 'Only a Girl'.

Her voice came out of the sound system clear and strong, soaring through the high notes and powerful in the emotional bits, yet soft and sweet right at the very end. Jade seemed to sing brilliantly, and there was no doubt that she had talent as an actress. But that voice wasn't her real voice, and as people were judging her on it, that wasn't fair. Did Jade know about the microphone, I wondered? I was sure that she did, because I knew Jade was as ruthless as she was ambitious. She wouldn't have the same kind of standards that Danny would have if he found out about how he was being manipulated. The microphone was probably even her idea.

When Danny finally came on the audience erupted. Banners were produced, fan clubs chanted and it took Brianna a long time to calm them down.

They played a video package of an interview with Danny where he talked about working on *Kensington Heights* and his brush with pop stardom. He talked about how he didn't think he stood a better chance than any of the other kids in the competition just because he was already well known and had had a number one single. I watched Danny on the big screen, his dark hair flopping into his eyes as he explained that talent was all that really counted in the end, and that either you had it or you didn't, and it was impossible to fake. He really meant that, I knew that he did.

I looked at Dakshima and crossed the fingers on both hands as Danny came out.

His song was 'Love Gets it Wrong Every Time'.

As he opened his mouth to sing the opening line, I held my breath. But I needn't have worried because the sound that came out of the speakers was wonderful, even better than the voice on his number one single. Apart from anything else you could hardly hear him because the moment he started his fans leapt to their feet and started screaming and cheering. A few of them even cried!

At the end, Mick Caruso looked Danny right in the eye and said, "You were on the money there, son. You can never hide true talent – and you've proved that."

Brianna turned to the camera and listed the numbers that the people at home had to call to register their votes, and then suddenly the credits were rolling and the studio relaxed. We had a forty-five minute break until the results show.

"You may go to the bathroom," Miss Baptista informed the chorus. "And then straight back. As you know, in the results show you will be singing with the winning leads, so I want you in your places looking bright as buttons in good time."

Most of us didn't move for a second. "Go! Go!" Carmen told us. "And no lingering!"

"No lingering?" Dakshima said, as we hurried to the toilets even though we didn't really want to go. "Who'd want to linger in a bog?"

As we stood in the queue Anne-Marie and Nydia raced up to me and hugged me – both at once, almost knocking me off of my feet.

"You won!" Nydia exclaimed happily.

"And now we're going to work together again," Anne-Marie said, kissing me and then Dakshima on the cheek. Wrinkling her nose, Dakshima wiped her hand across her cheek. She wasn't really a kissy-kissy sort of girl, but Anne-Marie was on such a high I was sure she didn't notice.

"Not for sure," Nydia reminded Anne-Marie, grimacing and crossing her fingers. "We might not both get through – and Jade was actually pretty good."

"Jade was rubbish – no sensible person would vote for her. So of course we'll get through," Anne-Marie said happily. "I was brilliant and so were you. I wonder what boys we'll get to play opposite us? Even Danny was really good tonight. All those singing lessons he's had have really paid off."

"Annie!" Nydia warned. "You're tempting fate."

"Nonsense," Anne-Marie said, spotting Sean at the end of the corridor. "I'm *making* fate. Positive thinking works every time. That's how come I've got *the* Sean Rivers as a boyfriend."

"Hey," Sean said, looking rather embarrassed to be greeting us in the line to the loo. "Well done, you guys!"

"Thanks, Sean," I said. "I still actually can't believe it – yay us!"

"And I was brilliant, wasn't I?" Anne-Marie told Sean happily.

"Yes, you were," Sean told Anne-Marie, winking at me so that Anne-Marie dug him playfully in the ribs.

"Everyone was really good. Danny and Jade have really been working hard."

"It could have been you, you know," Anne-Marie said, smiling at Sean. "You could have wiped the floor with those boys out there, even Danny."

"Me?" Sean laughed. "Have you *ever* heard me sing?"

"Well, no," Anne-Marie said. "I suppose not."

"And there's reason for that. I am a dreadful singer."

Sean's laugh echoed down the corridor and an entire queue of girls who had been trying really hard to act cool nearly melted into one massive puddle on the floor.

"Come on," Anne-Marie said, taking Sean's hand. "Let's go and get something to drink. I'm parched. And by the way, I bet you could sing if you tried..." Anne-Marie blew us a kiss as she towed her boyfriend away, watched by a dozen wistful girls.

"*That* was Sean Rivers," Talitha said, dreamy eyed.

"He is soooo cute," Hannah sighed.

"Pull it together, girls," Dakshima said. "He's only a guy, after all!"

"A guy your bedroom walls are a shrine to," Talitha said.

"Anyway," Dakshima said, firmly turning to Nydia, "I wish we were allowed to have our mobiles because I'd vote for you right now."

"Don't worry," Nydia said. "My mum's got the whole

of our family promising to vote at least five times, and I've got a big family!"

Just as we were nearing the door of the ladies loo, Danny walked up the corridor. He saw me and I saw him, and then we both looked at something else – him at the floor and me at the picture of the stick lady on the toilet door. *Typical I should see him now*, I thought furiously.

Only Danny didn't walk past me, he stopped.

I looked at Dakshima whose brows were sky high, and then with some effort I looked at Danny. "Hi," I said.

"Hi," Danny said, glancing at Dakshima and the other queuing girls, who were open-mouthed from first seeing Sean Rivers and now Danny Harvey in the flesh. "Could I have a word?"

I considered my position. I'd been in the queue for so long that I now actually did need to go, but while I was happily able to chat to Sean, there was no way that I could speak to Danny in the line for the loo. I'd just have to hold on.

"OK," I said, stepping out of the line. "See you in a minute," I said to Dakshima as I followed Danny a little further down the corridor.

"Congratulations, by the way," Danny said. "On getting in the chorus. It seems that you can't quite leave show business alone after all."

"Danny, I—" I began defensively.

"That's not what I wanted to say," Danny interrupted. "I want to say sorry for the other night. For assuming you'd come round to tell me you still liked me. I mean, of course you don't still like me. I behaved like a right idiot. And I'm sorry about that too, but I wanted you to know that I really haven't let *Kensington Heights*, the number one single or anything go to my head, not really. I'm still me and I always will be, even if I get this part."

I looked at him for a long moment. "I know you're still you," I said. "And I'm sorry too for stomping off like that."

"So why did you come over?" Danny asked me.

"I..." There was absolutely no way I could tell him the truth. Not after he'd made such a sweet speech telling me that he was still him. How could I say, "Actually, no, you're not you, you're a fake, only you don't know it."

"I came round because I thought it would be nice to say hi, wish you good luck, that sort of thing," I told him.

"That's really nice to know," Danny said. "That's... really nice."

"Well, good luck then," I said.

"Thanks, Ruby," Danny said. "See you around."

I raced back to the toilet to find the queue almost gone, as Carmen Baptista appeared at the end of the corridor and called for us all to go back and take our places. The results were in.

This time, as the twelve finalists stood on their mark, there was tense and scary *dum-de-dum* music, which sounded like the beat of a heart on the verge of an attack. Brianna told everyone how many votes had been cast and that it had been a really close run thing. And then she prepared to announce which four finalists had won the lead parts in *Spotlight! The Musical*.

"And the winner who will play the part of Serena is..."

"If she waits any longer I'll have turned fourteen," Dakshima whispered to me half way through the gigantic pause.

"Anne-Marie Chance!" Brianna read out. Anne-Marie leapt up about two metres in the air and screamed her head off in a most unladylike fashion. She skipped over to Brianna and waited as Brianna prepared to announce who would be playing opposite Anne-Marie.

"The part of Jake goes to... David Rubenfeld!" Massive cheers from the crowd.

I held my breath as I waited to see who would get the role of Arial. Maybe it wouldn't be Jade. I still hoped and prayed that Nydia's name would be called out.

The pause before Brianna read out the name seemed to go one forever. Then...

"Jade Caruso!"

My eyes darted over to Nydia, who dropped her head for a second before squaring her shoulders and smiling again.

"How did Nydia not win that?" Talitha said, unable to contain herself despite feeling Carmen's watchful eyes on us. "She was the best singer by miles! What's wrong with people?"

"It's down to the public vote I suppose," Dakshima said, glancing uneasily at me. "She should have won it. She blew Jade away."

Finally Brianna announced the part of Sebastian. The heartbeat tension music was ramped up another level and this time Brianna's pause seemed to go on for all eternity.

Finally she read out, "Danny Harvey!" and was drowned out by the rapturous applause.

As happy as I was for Danny, I found it hard to join in. Maybe it was wrong, but I could have taken the cheating if Nydia *and* Anne-Marie had got a part, but Nydia hadn't. And it just wasn't fair that she should lose out to a fake performance. And I was sure that if the voters at home knew that then they'd feel the same way.

"And finally," Brianna said, "all that remains is for our winning chorus to sing us out with our four new leads, with the theme song from the show *Spotlight!* We'll see you all again in a month for the charity premiere performance of *Spotlight!* right here in this studio. And don't forget to catch up with the behind the scenes show bringing you all the action and gossip from the rehearsals – *Spotlight!: Change the Bulb* every weeknight at 5 p.m." Brianna gestured at us all, waiting on our marks to sing the closing number. "Take it away guys…!"

"I'm really glad our choir has won the competition and everything," I whispered to Dakshima out of the corner of my mouth under the swell of the music. "But I never imagined I'd end up singing in a chorus on stage with my worst enemy and ex-boyfriend."

"Must be all that positive thinking you've been doing," Dakshima said. "Like Anne-Marie says, it always pays off in the end."

We sang the final song and as soon as Carmen let us leave the set, I raced off to find Nydia. I had to tell her everything so that she wouldn't feel so bad.

"Where are you going?" Dakshima chased after me, catching my arm. I told her my plan.

"Don't do that," Dakshima said.

"What? Why not – we have to sort this out *now*," I

protested. "We can't pretend we don't know any more, Dakshima. Not now."

"OK," Dakshima said. "Maybe you're right. We do have to find some way to sort this out. But if we tell Nydia and she tells her mum and dad, what do you think is going to happen? They'll find a way to make it look like we got it wrong or that we're making it up. You and I are the only two people who know we know the truth and we need to keep it that way, for now anyway."

"What shall we do then?" I asked her, anxiously.

"I don't know yet," Dakshima said. "But we've got just over four weeks of rehearsal ahead. We'll think of something. I promise."

SPOTLIGHT! THE MUSICAL©

LYRICS AND MUSIC BY MICK CARUSO
BOOK BY DEN FELTON

ACT ONE
SCENE TWO

Int. Day. The Rehearsal room at The School of Performing Arts. ARIAL enters stage right, picks up a bag she had forgotten. Turning she sees SEBASTIAN practising at the barre. Their eyes meet and there is an awkward moment.

> **SEBASTIAN**
> Arial, I didn't see you there.

> **ARIAL**
> (Holding up bag.)
> I forgot my bag.

SEBASTIAN

(Walks to centre stage.)
Are you OK after today's
lesson? Mrs Kaminski was
pretty tough on you.

ARIAL

I'm OK, it's just hard, I
guess, being the new girl.
Compared to all of you, I
feel like such an amateur.

SEBASTIAN

(Taking a couple of steps
nearer.) That's crazy talk.
You won a scholarship to be
here. You deserve this more
than anyone else because
you've already proved how
talented you are.

ARIAL

Do you really think so?

SEBASTIAN

(Taking Arial's hand.)

Sure. Listen…

(Cue intro music to 'STARLIGHT
DREAMS')

Chapter Twelve

Dakshima's dad took us to our first full day of rehearsals the Saturday after the live show. The rehearsal rooms were around the corner from the TV studios.

Spotlight! was written with hardly any sets or complex scenes to learn. Mick Caruso hoped that after all the publicity from the TV premiere it would be performed in every school across the country, and the rights income he earned from that would add to his millions. If it really took off big time, he planned to make a movie of it the following year.

Because we were all under sixteen there were only so many hours of rehearsal we were allowed to do before the TV premiere. Two afternoons after school during the week, and one full day at the weekend. David Rubenfeld, who normally lived in Scotland, was staying in a hotel with one of his parents, and a tutor to keep him up to speed with his schoolwork. As the rest of us lived in London, we got to keep going to our normal schools and living at home. We were all a bit miffed about that as we wouldn't have minded staying in a hotel and ordering pizza and fries on room service.

What I wasn't prepared for as I walked into the rehearsal room was the camera crew. "Why are they here?" I asked Anne-Marie, who had already arrived and was stretching her legs at the barre.

"Another TV spin off," Anne-Marie said. "They're filming us to see if a bunch of kids can really perform a brand new musical live on TV after only a month of rehearsal. I expect they'll be trying to create loads of tension and hoping we cry. But I'm not going to. Why would I? I've done school plays that are harder than this. All the minor roles are already cast and they've been rehearsing for weeks. All we've got to do is slot in and outshine them. Easy."

I looked across the large, light, mirrored room to where a group of actors I hadn't seen before eyed us suspiciously.

"Is that them?" I asked.

Anne-Marie nodded. "They don't like us at the moment. They think we are a bunch of amateurs who don't deserve our parts. Us, Ruby, *amateurs*? You go and ask how many of *them* have made a Hollywood movie – go on."

"I'd rather not," I said. "And besides, none of us have

done anything like this before, not professionally. I haven't even done it at school. I never got picked for musicals."

I glanced over that the film crew and was dismayed to see that the camera was pointed directly at Anne-Marie and me.

So far through this whole experience no one had seemed to notice that ex-child star Ruby Parker was in Highgate Comprehensive school choir, which just went to show, I supposed, how very ordinary I was when everyone wasn't looking out for me.

I'd asked Mr Petrelli to just fill my name in on the form as R. Parker. And in the edited highlights they showed at the live final, the director focused on Dakshima and Adele. And after the show had wrapped, while I was waiting for Mum, Jeremy and Dad to bring the car round, I heard two ladies whispering behind me.

"Didn't she used to be someone?" I heard one say.

"Possibly," the other whispered back.

"Maybe my cousin Jenny," the first one said.

"That'll be it," the second one said. "If she was someone, I'd have remembered."

So that proved it. The moment I took myself out of the limelight I was instantly forgettable. Not Like Sean, who had been retried for much longer than me and still had fan letters flooding in. People still missed him, magazines still talked about him. That was because he was a proper star. I wasn't, I was just Ruby Parker, the girl who accidentally got famous for a bit.

Besides, I knew about behind the scenes shows like this. They made one of *Kensington Heights* when I was Angel MacFarley on it, and they'd set up my screen mum, Brett Summers, to look as if she kept a large bottle of vodka in her dressing room that she drank between takes.

The crew would always be working an angle, looking for a "journey" taken by one of the participants. Searching for characters that the audience at home could root for or despise. It didn't matter what you were really like, with a few clever questions and a bit of editing, they could make you seem any way they wanted to.

They would have researched all they could about every single person here and, as I was fairly sure that I was the only one that had been in a TV soap, made a film, and run away from Hollywood because I couldn't stand the pressure, it was only a matter of time before they sought me out.

Carmen Baptista still hadn't arrived when a blonde woman from the camera crew jogged across the rehearsal room to where I was standing with Anne-Marie.

"Hi, Ruby," she said, holding out her hand. "I'm Clara Robson, one of the producers on *Spotlight!: Change the Bulb*. We didn't realise until today that the R. Parker on the list was *the* Ruby Parker. It's so great you're part of this, viewers will be thrilled to know that you haven't disappeared from their lives forever. We'd love to talk to you about your career and why you've decided to make your comeback in this way."

"I'm not coming back," I said, as Carmen Baptista walked in. "I'm in a school choir that won a competition. That's it."

"And that's great, just the thing that we're looking for. Come on, Ruby, you know the score – this will really boost your profile, get you back out there again. The last year or so must have been hard. Parents divorcing, leaving *Kensington Heights*, making that dud film – what was it called? And all that business in Hollywood, your mother dating Jeremy Fort. How does that make you feel?"

"Take your places please!" Carmen told us, her voice echoing off the floor to ceiling mirrors.

"How about we have a chat at lunch break?" Clara persisted.

I sighed and looked at Anne-Marie, whose lips were pursed in disapproval. Whether it was because Clara was talking to me or because she was *not* talking to Anne-Marie, I wasn't sure.

"Look, Clara, you may have the right to film me as part of the chorus, but to interview me specifically you need my mother's permission and you don't have it. And seeing as I'm not going to ask her to give it to you, and there's no way she would anyway even if I wanted her to, there's no point in wasting your time. I don't want to talk to you."

Clara's eyes narrowed. "So it's true – you've become a right little diva," she said cruelly. "How the mighty have fallen."

"I do not come here to waste my time," Carmen Baptista shouted behind us. "I count to five only. One…"

"Well it was bound to happen," Anne-Marie said, as we joined a line at the back of the room. "If you really wanted to be left alone you should have done what my Sean did, and laid low at school. You have to admit, Ruby, your plans to stay away from showbiz didn't exactly last."

"I know," I said, "but I didn't plan this… I don't even understand how or why."

"That's because you're thirteen," Anne-Marie told me. "It'll be easier to deal with when you're my age. Oh, look out, here comes Danny and Jade, and they are late."

I watched as Jade entered with Danny at her side. Danny looked embarrassed and a little worried. Jade, on the other hand, didn't seem to mind at all.

"You are LATE!" Carmen Baptista shouted angrily. "I do not tolerate lateness!"

"Sorry, Miss Baptista," Danny said. "There was traffic and...'

"Traffic?" Carmen Baptista nearly spat out the word. "Was there not traffic for everybody else in this room and did we not get here on time? There is *never* any excuse to be late."

"Excuse me," said Jade, putting her hand on her hip and cocking her head to one side. "Do you know who I am?"

"I do not care who you are," Carmen Baptista said. "Except that you are late."

"I am your boss's daughter," Jade said snootily. "And I don't think that you should speak to me that way, otherwise you might find yourself out of a job."

Carmen Baptista stared at Jade, her black eyes glittering with fury.

"Your father paid me ten times my usual fee to leave the production I choreographed in New York, to come here and save this show from certain failure. Your father *begged* me to come. And if you do not show me the same respect that your father has, *little girl*," she growled, "then it will have to be you who tells your father that Carmen Baptista walked out of this fiasco because she could not tolerate his spoilt little brat. Perhaps we should get him down here now and tell him why I am quitting. Would you like that?"

Jade stared at Carmen Baptista for a second longer, then she said something in such a low voice I couldn't hear it, but I assumed it was, "Sorry I'm late, Miss Baptista, it won't happen again."

Because then, with her cheeks burning, she'd tossed her hair over her shoulders and went and stood next to Danny in the front row of the waiting cast and chorus members.

"Silence!" Carmen Baptista yelled at us even though we were all perfectly quiet. "Because of lateness we now only have twenty minutes to warm up. Before we start I want you to remember something. You are not here to enjoy yourself. You are not here to make friends. You are here to work, because it's my reputation that is on the line and I will not have it compromised. Be most sure, if you don't come up to scratch then you will be leaving. I don't care what competition you won, how many people voted for you or who your father is. Is that understood?"

We all mumbles "yes", shuffling and nodding, glancing nervously at each other.

"IS THAT UNDERSTOOD?" Miss Baptista yelled.

"Yes, Miss Baptista!" we chorused as one, loud and clear.

As we stretched and warmed up our bodies, I whispered to Anne-Marie out of the corner of my mouth. "How has Nydia been this week? I haven't seen her since Sunday. She sounds all chirpy and fine, but is she really?"

"She's the same with me," Anne-Marie told me as she stretched out her calves. "She acts all fine, but she knows that her voice was miles better than that Jade's and even mine. She should have won a part, and knowing she didn't because people at home didn't like her enough – that's a pretty harsh thing to deal with."

"It's more than harsh," I said, bending forward to stretch my hamstring muscles as I glanced over at Jade. "It's not fair."

"But that's show business, isn't it?" Anne-Marie said. "It is harsh and it's not fair. That's what Sylvia Lighthouse is always telling us. Nydia understands that."

"Yes but this time it really isn't..."

"You two at the back!" Carmen Baptista yelled at us. Everyone stopped what they were doing and looked at us, including Jade, who was smirking.

"Come forward," Carmen Baptista instructed us.

Anne-Marie and I filed reluctantly through the rows.

"What did I say? Did you not hear me? Are you deaf?"

Anne-Marie and I shook our head.

"You are in a working rehearsal, not the playground, and while you are here I expect you to do as you are told and work."

"Sorry, Miss Baptista," Anne-Marie and I said together.

"Good, now drop and give me ten!" Carmen Baptista bellowed.

"Ten what?" Anne-Marie asked, confused.

"Ten press-ups of course, you imbecile!" Carmen Baptista shouted right in Anne-Marie's face. Someone behind us sniggered, but one look from Miss Baptista shut them right up.

Anne-Marie looked at me and, shrugging, dropped to the floor and started to do her press-ups.

"I've never done a press-up before," I said hesitantly.

"Now you learn," Carmen Baptista growled. "Right now, or I'll double them."

It came as an enormous relief when we realised that we would mostly be rehearsed by Carmen Baptista's assistant, Tristan Blanc – to begin with, at least. Miss

Baptista would come in after we'd learnt the steps, songs and directions, and then polish us up like diamonds, as she put it.

Tristan was much less frightening than Miss Baptista, younger and really funny, so that half the time we were having such a good time that we forgot we were learning dance steps and song parts. As part of the chorus I didn't have any lines to learn. What we did was come in on the big dance numbers and crowd scenes. But I had been helping Anne-Marie learn her character Serena's lines after school, so I was getting to know the script pretty well anyway. Compared to some scripts I'd had to learn for *Kensington Heights* and *Hollywood High*, it was fairly easy.

"Mr Caruso wants you all miked up from the beginning," Tristan explained as sound engineers came round and hooked us all up. "He says he wants you to get used to listening to your voice through the sound system. It's not the norm in theatre, but I guess as this is a TV special it's the right thing to do. Anyway Mr Caruso is the boss, so we do his bidding."

As the tiny microphones were attached to our heads with a bit of invisible tape just below our hair lines, I noticed that Jade and Danny's microphones looked just a little bit different to the others. And I couldn't be sure, but it seemed to me that their voices came out of different speakers. It had to be the Auto-tune Miracle Microphones. Mick didn't want anyone to ever hear Danny and Jade's real voices, and by insisting that we all used microphones from the start, he could make sure that didn't happen. He had everything covered to protect his daughter.

The musical itself was quite simple to learn. It was the story of Arial, a girl from a poor background who wins a scholarship to a very exclusive stage school, leaving her family behind. Once there she battles against the prejudices of her classmates, including the fierce and feisty Serena, survives the extremely strict staff and makes friends with Jake. Finally she finds herself, falls in love with Sebastian, and *then* finds fame in the spotlight, which temporarily changes her into a not such nice person, before Sebastian reminds her what friendship truly means and everyone is happy again.

While Tristan was teaching us the big dance numbers, I really enjoyed myself. I almost forgot about how unfair it was that Nydia hadn't won a part in the show and for a couple hours I didn't think about Danny and Jade's Auto-tune Miracle Microphones at all. It just felt good to be in the atmosphere of a rehearsal room again, with that smell and those sounds and all of the feelings that I hadn't realised I missed so much.

It was almost lunchtime when Carmen Baptista came in, just as we were finishing our third run through of the biggest number in the second act. She stood by the door and crossed her arms as she watched us.

"You," she said, pointing at me. I looked over my shoulder. "Yes, you. Step forward please."

I did as she asked me, unsure what I had done wrong, but completely certain that my arms couldn't take ten more press-ups.

"You're not trained as a dancer, are you?" she asked.

"Not really, Miss Baptista," I said apologetically. "I've had a bit of basic ballet training. I'm sorry."

"Hmph," she snorted. "You move well, considering. With training and hard work you could be good. But you must work."

"OK," I squeaked, looking over my shoulder at Dakshima.

"The rest of you," she hollered, diverting her attention from me at last, "are a disgrace. If you do not improve by this afternoon, I fire you all!"

She smiled sweetly at Tristan and then stormed out.

"OK," Tristan said, clapping his hands together. "Let's break for lunch."

"So, Ruby," Clara Robson found me as I was eating lunch with Dakshima. "Had a chance to think about what we discussed earlier?"

"I thought I had thought about it?" I said, slurping a spoonful of soup.

"Come on, Ruby," Clara said. "It must have been pretty traumatic for you, all that business in Hollywood, especially at thirteen. Didn't it feel as if everyone had turned against you? That must have been hard to deal with. But we can help you raise your profile again."

I stood up abruptly. "Please, just leave me alone," I entreated before walking off down the corridor.

"Finding it hard to adjust to being a nobody, Ruby?" I head Jade call after me as I headed into the loos.

"Are you OK?" Anne-Marie asked, when she and Dakshima found me a few minutes later, splashing cold water on my face.

"I'm fine," I said crossly. "Just irritated that's all."

"Don't worry," Anne-Marie said, putting her hand on my shoulder. "Soon the criers will start breaking out and there will be drama all over the place for them to film."

"Anyway, I thought you handled her really well,"

Dakshima added. "I'd have probably spilled my guts and worried about it later. Lucky that I'm a total nobody."

"I suppose growing up in TV and film has got something going for it," I smiled. "At least now I've finally learnt how to handle journalists and nosey producers."

"I've got to get back," Anne-Marie said. "I'm helping David with some tricky dance steps. See you in five."

"Ruby," Dakshima said, once we were alone, "do you really think the show will be any good?"

"It'll be fine," I said. "It will be great – but the question is, *should* it be? Perhaps we should tell Clara Robson about the microphones."

"And what will happen?" Dakshima asked me. "All of the people that do deserve a chance – which includes you and me by the way – won't get it. No, there has to be some way we can make sure the show goes on *and* expose what's happening."

"And what about Danny?" I asked her.

"What about him?" she said.

"I don't want to make a fool of him. We'd have to tell him before we did anything. And I don't know if I can."

"Then perhaps we shouldn't say anything," Dakshima said thoughtfully. "In a couple of months this will all be over and will it still really matter then?"

* * *

It was Jeremy who came to pick us up that evening, or rather, Jeremy's chauffer driving one of his Rolls Royces. Anne-Marie, Dakshima and I all climbed into the back where Jeremy was waiting for us. "How was it, girls?" he asked with a smile.

"It was good," I said, trying not to feel guilty. "I really enjoyed it."

"I was fabulous," Anne-Marie said. "And the rest of my cast are pretty good too – you know, good enough so as not to bring my talent down, but not so great that they outshine me."

"How lovely for you," Dakshima said, winking at me.

"I know," Anne-Marie said blithely.

"My favourite part of putting on a production for the stage is the rehearsal time," Jeremy said. "Working as part of a team to bring everything together. Labouring over something you truly love to make it as good as it can be. Those are the golden moments in any actor's career."

"Really?" Dakshima asked him. "Not the bit where everyone claps and you know that the whole world loves you?"

"Well, yes," Jeremy admitted. "Applause is music to

any actor's ears, but it's the craft that's important, Dakshima, the craft. Don't you agree, Ruby?"

I nodded, thinking once again about Danny and Jade and how they were cheating the craft, whether they knew it or not.

"I suppose I always enjoy making something much more than I've enjoyed watching it," I said. "But I've never done live theatre before so I don't really know what it's like to hear applause."

"You wait," Anne-Marie said, smiling. "You wait until you're out on that stage in front of a real audience. *Then* we'll see if you give up acting for good."

When we got in Mum was sitting at the kitchen table staring into space and smiling for no particular reason. She did that a lot recently and it was weird to see how much she smiled when she was truly happy. For a long time before she and Dad broke up, she hardly ever smiled at all. It was nice to see her so happy, but I was sad too because only now did I realise how unhappy she'd been for so long.

"Hello, love," she said, as I walked in and dumped my kit bag on the table.

Jeremy bent over and kissed her on the cheek. "I've just got a couple of calls to make to the States before dinner," he said. "I'll leave you two girls to it."

"Take that off the table, dinner's ready," Mum said,

nodding at my bag as she got up. "I've made your favourite."

"Mmm, great," I said. "I'm starving."

"I thought you would be," Mum smiled. "How was the rehearsal?"

"It was great, Mum, really great," I said. "But..."

"But what, Ruby?" Mum asked, looking up from the hob.

"I'm enjoying it ever so much but I... I don't know if I should," I said finally.

"Why ever not? You left the Academy to go to a normal school, and now you're in the chorus of a televised world premiere of a musical! It sounds like a plot from *Kensington Heights* – *and* a dream come true."

"I just wish Nydia had got through..." I said, dropping my head.

"Oh, love," Mum said, "I know she's your friend, but it's not your fault she didn't win the vote. Besides, she won't want you to miss out because she has – Nydia's not that sort of girl. You're going round there after tea, aren't you? I'm sure you'll say something that will cheer her up."

"I know, it's just..."

"What is it?" Mum asked me gently.

"Mum, if you knew something that was really bad

and wrong, but that if you told people about it, it would mess up something that was really good for a lot of people and hurt someone you care about, what would you do?"

"Are you in trouble, Ruby?" Mum asked.

"No," I told her. "No, it's... it's part of the plot of the show. I'm just wondering what you would do. It's sort of... homework."

"Well, the truth always comes out in the end, Ruby," Mum said. "I'd tell whatever it was to whoever I had to, to make things right again. The longer you leave a lie, the worse it gets."

"Right," I said. That was exactly what I had expected Mum to say. But hearing it didn't make it any easier to do.

"Go and wash your hands and then you can set the table." Mum said. "I want you back from Nydia's by nine-thirty."

"You *can* talk about it you know," Nydia said, after half an hour of all of us sitting around at her house nattering over the DVD we were supposed to be watching.

"Talk about what?" Anne-Marie asked. "Hey, how's Greg? When's he coming down next?"

"When we start filming the next series of *Totally Busted*," Nydia said. "We've got some really cool pranks coming up, but they're top secret so I can't tell you about them, which means you will have talk to me about your rehearsals. I'm not going to burst into tears or anything.

"No one thought you were going to," Sean said with a slow smile. "It's just that Annie hasn't stopped talking about them all day and I'm so over it."

"Sean!" Anne-Marie punched him on the shoulder, then turned to Nydia. "We don't want to upset you."

"I'm not upset!" Nydia exclaimed. "All right, I am a bit, but I'll get over it. How long would I last in acting if I didn't get over rejection? Being an actor is mostly getting rejected, as Ms Lighthouse is always telling us."

"Has anyone noticed that Ms Lighthouse hardly ever says anything cheerful?" Sean observed through a mouthful of popcorn.

"Rehearsals are fine," I said. "Especially for us lot in the chorus because all the stuff we have to do is dead easy."

"And even though my character isn't the actual lead as *such*, she is actually far more interesting than Jade's wimpy old character, so I'd say I had the most interesting part to learn any day of the week," Anne-Marie observed.

"You should have won that vote though, Nyds," I said because I couldn't help myself. "It's so wrong you didn't – you were better than anyone else on that stage."

"You were," Anne-Marie agreed. "You beat me."

Nydia paused for a moment and then shrugged. "I guess the public just didn't like me the best," she said.

"Well, the public are idiots, everyone knows that," Anne-Marie said.

"Yeah, they voted *her* in," Sean said, nodding at Anne-Marie and earning himself another punch. "But the main thing is you totally rocked it on national TV and everyone who's anyone saw that, plus everyone here likes you the best and that's what really counts. Life in the spotlight is hardly ever as good as you think it's going to be. And in a few weeks time the show will be finished, but you will still be you and we will still be us."

"Only slightly more famous," Anne-Marie said, making Nydia laugh.

"Look, I'm a bit down about it," she said, "but I still want you to talk about the show and what it's like. I want all the gossip about Jade and if she's got her claws into Danny yet. So tell me all about it, OK?"

"Oh, where to begin?" Anne-Marie asked, gleefully. "So, about that over-rated diva…"

"I thought we'd already talked about you?" I said.

This time it was me who got punched on the shoulder.

In bed later that night, I was about to switch my lamp off when I heard my mobile ring. I was not allowed to answer calls on it after 9 p.m. but I picked it up anyway, just in case it was Nydia and she needed an emergency pep talk after all. But it wasn't Nydia's number flashing up on my phone. It was Danny's. I hesitated for a second, then I answered it.

"Hello?" I said, trying to sound like I didn't know who it was.

"Hey, Ruby, it's me… it's Danny."

"Oh, hi," I said in my best casual voice.

"We didn't get a chance to talk today," Danny said.

"Well you have your part to learn and I have… dancing about to do," I said.

"How do you think it's going?" Danny asked.

"Really well," I said stiffly.

"Look, I'm sorry if you don't want to talk to me," Danny said.

"No, it's not that. I do…." I trailed off as I tried to work out what to say. "It's just a bit odd. I don't know *how* to talk to you any more. I'm a bit rusty."

"Me too," Danny said. "Look, not that you'll care or anything, but I'm not going out with Melody any more."

"Oh?" I said, failing to sound uninterested.

"She said there was no way I should have got through to the finals when she hadn't and that if I won a lead part that it would be a joke. So that pretty much finished us off, which I don't mind really because it turned out she wasn't really a lot of fun."

"Well, never mind," I said. "There are plenty more fish in the sea."

There was second or two of silence, and then Danny and I burst out laughing.

"This is silly," Danny said, his voice warm in my ear. "If we're out of practise talking to each other, then let's make sure we talk to each other a lot more, OK?"

"OK," I said, smiling. "I'd like that."

"See you at rehearsal on Tuesday?" Danny asked me.

"It's a date," I said. "Though obviously not an *actual* date."

There was another moment of silence and then Danny said, "Goodbye" and hung up.

"Not an *actual* date," I repeated to myself as I switched off my lamp. "I can't believe I just said that."

It took me along time to get to sleep.

Meet the girls that you helped put in the spotlight as we talk exclusively to Jade Caruso and Anne-Marie Chance, the UK's newest and youngest leading ladies!

tg: Wow, girls, you must all feel like you are living a dream?

jc: Well, I know I do. I just feel so privileged that the British public picked me to be in my dad's show. And I am glad I made Dad put me through the auditions just like everyone else.

amc: It goes to show that what really matters is your talent and not who you know, although a lot of really talented kids didn't make it through to the final.

tg: Neither of you girls have previously had lead roles in either TV or film – how does that make you feel?

amc: I feel it's about time, I've been waiting for my big break for *ages*!

jc: It makes *me* feel amazingly proud and lucky, of course, and a little bit scared too. I'm determined to give it my best shot.

tg: Jade, has the fact that you're Mick Caruso's daughter given you any problems with your other cast members?

jc: I think the fact that I won the public vote against some pretty stiff competition shows that I earned my role. But everyone has been wonderful. Anne-Marie and the other girls in the chorus are like my sisters now, which is great because my real sister is a total pain in the neck!

tg: What about the leading lads? Jade is lucky enough to have Teen Girl fave Danny Harvey all to herself, so tell us, Anne-Marie, is David Rubenfeld just as cute?

amc: He's easily as cute as Danny Harvey any day of the week.

jc: And like Danny he really is a great performer, which is far more important than how a person looks, even if he is pretty cute.

amc: Yes, David and I do make a talented pair.

jc: It's great to have such strong support for mine and Danny's starring roles.

tg: The opening night is not far away now. Are you nervous?

amc: Not remotely. Why would I be? I rock!

jc: A few jitters are healthy and I know I'm very nervous. There would be nothing worse than letting over-confidence and arrogance catch you out on the night. It would let down all the people that were kind enough to vote.

We at *Teen Girl!* have a very special prize for you to win and that's ten – count 'em, *ten!* – pairs of VIP tickets to see the TV premiere of *Spotlight! The Musical* among an audience of top celebrities. Just answer this question.

Which former child star is now finding her feet in the chorus of *Spotlight!*?

Text or e-mail your answers FREE to the usual address by twelve noon on Friday! Good luck!

Chapter Thirteen

"Well that's just typical of the press," Anne-Marie said, flinging Dakshima's copy of *Teen Girl!* down during our break at Saturday's rehearsal. "They twisted everything I said to make me look shallow and Jade look all lovely and nice."

"So you didn't say any of that stuff?" Dakshima asked, retrieving the magazine and smoothing it out.

"I said it, but not in the way they printed it. I was being light-hearted and jokey." She sniffed a little. "When you see it on the page it makes me look like a right cow!"

"Well, it *is* kind of hard to print jokeyness, I imagine," I said. "You should have asked them to print stage directions, like in a script. Anyway, never mind your humiliation, what about *mine*? Did you see that competition question?"

"Oh, yeah, that was Jade's idea," Anne-Marie said. "Told the journalist she wanted everyone to know how talented even the chorus was. Yeah, right."

"Typical Jade," I sighed. "That's just the catty sort of thing she would do to get at me. I thought her ignoring me for the last couple of weeks was too easy."

"Just forget about it," Anne-Marie said. "We've got more important things to worry about. Miss Baptista and Mick are going to watch our first full rehearsal in the TV studio today. And the behind-the-scenes film crew are going crazy trying to stir up things up."

"Doesn't look like they'll have to do that much stirring between you and Jade," Dakshima grinned.

"You can't believe everything you read!" Anne-Marie exclaimed. "Even if it *is* technically true..."

"Hi, Ruby." Danny stopped by our table, his cheeks flaring as each we all stared at him.

"And 'hi, Anne-Marie and Dakshima' too," Anne-Marie said. "Or have we become invisible?"

"Hi, Danny," I replied, shooting Anne-Marie a 'button it or else' look.

"I was just going to hang around outside for a bit and I wondered if you wanted to... hang about too," Danny faltered.

Dakshima snorted into her drink and Anne-Marie hastily picked up the discarded copy of *Teen Girl!* and held it up in front of her face. I could see her shoulders shaking with laughter.

"Thanks, I could do with some fresh air actually," I said, kicking Anne-Marie under the table hard enough to make her yelp. "See you in a couple of minutes, girls."

Once outside, standing next to the wheely bins Danny laughed, his shoulder relaxing.

"That wasn't my coolest moment," he said. "I sounded like a right idiot. I've been trying to talk to you on your own all day, but I couldn't work out how."

"Well, it worked," I smiled, hugging myself against the chill of the cold afternoon. "I'm here now so – what did you want to say to me?"

Danny looked at me for a moment as if I had just asked him the most terrifying question he had ever heard.

"Nothing really," he said. "I just wanted us to talk. You know, so that we can be cool around each other again..."

"Oh, right," I said, trying hard to hide my disappointment. Ever since that late night phone conversation I'd thought that maybe, *just maybe*, he might asked me out again, and once I'd allowed myself to think about it I realised that I wouldn't mind much if he did. In fact I'd really like it.

We'd chatted a few times since then, in the corridors at rehearsals and once after school when I bumped into him on the way home. Each time it always seemed that he was on the verge of saying something else, but didn't. I had hoped that by now he might have decided what it was.

If Danny asked me out and if I said yes (obviously I would) then not only would I be really happy, I'd be able to tell him about the Auto-tune Miracle Microphone and he wouldn't hate me. Because he'd realise I was doing the right thing and trying to help him. Dakshima assured me that she was working on plan of how to fix everything without wrecking the show for everyone else, but I had absolutely no idea how she could.

"What do you think Mick Caruso and Miss Baptista will think of the show today?" I asked Danny.

"Honestly? I'm not sure we're ready yet. There's only a week to go before the live TV performance and I think Miss Baptista's going to be shouting at us for most of it. I keep forgetting my dance moves and Jade can't seem to remember half the words to the songs!"

"You're probably right," I said, thinking how Anne-Marie said that rehearsing with Miss Baptista was like joining a showbusiness army. "But considering most of the cast has never done anything like this before and that we're all really, really trying, I'm not sure we're going to be any better than we are at this point."

"There's still a week to go," Danny smiled. "A lot can

happen in a week. And I don't think that Miss Baptista will really throw any of us off the show."

"Especially not Jade," I said. "Even if she can't remember all of her lines after nearly a month of rehearsals."

"She's learnt them. I've helped her," Danny said, making me look up sharply. "I've got to know her a lot better in these last few weeks and it's the nerves that get her." He blushed. "You know, I even have to kiss her in the show, which is a bit weird. But once you get to know her you realise she's actually quite a laugh. I think all that snotty harsh stuff she pulls is really to cover up how shy she is. Everyone knows how hard she's worked and her voice is sounding really great."

"Maybe..." I said, unconvinced but unable to tell Danny why.

"Come on, Rube," Danny said, shortening my name in a way he hadn't since we split up. "Don't be so harsh. You, of everyone, should know how that feels."

"I do," I sighed, unable to look him in the eye. "Well, we'd better get back."

"Yes, we had," Danny said. Without warning he reached out and took my hand in his. I think I would have dropped dead on the spot, if it wasn't for the fact that I had to keep my heart beating just so I could hear what he was going to say next. "It's really great getting to know you again, Ruby Parker. I've really missed hanging out with you."

"Really? Because—" I didn't know what I wanted to say and I never got the chance to find out.

"Danny! There you are!" Danny dropped my hand as Jade came and put her arm around him, squeezing him hard and grinning at me. "Tristan wants us all back for our last rehearsal before we head off to the TV studio, and you know I really want to do my best for Daddy, so I need you now." She eyed me disdainfully. "And the last thing we need is to be held up by the chorus."

"I'm coming..." I began, as Jade walked off with Danny, her arm clamped around his shoulders. He didn't even look back. I trailed behind cluelessly. A minute ago I would have been approximately ninety-seven per cent sure that Danny still liked me, but now I wondered if he was actually about to tell me that he was going to ask Jade out. Stranger things have happened. Jade was very pretty after all, and it she'd apparently been showing Danny her nicer side – even if it was a side based wholly on lies and deceit.

I sighed and tried to shake the idea way. After all, nothing had really changed. I hadn't been going out with Danny before lunch, and I wasn't going out with Danny after lunch either.

So why did I feel as if something that should have happened hadn't?

Danny was chatting with the boys from the chorus as I walked back in the rehearsal room and Jade was waiting for me. She stepped in front of me and backed me out into the empty corridor.

"Stay away from him," she said very quietly. She may have been smiling with her mouth but her eyes looked deadly.

"*What*?" I said, drawing myself up to my fullest height, which was still a couple of centimetres shorter than Jade. "Are you seriously trying to warn me off being friends with Danny?"

Jade looked me up and down and barked one short hard laugh. "I'm not warning you, I'm *telling* you and I'm doing you a favour. Anyone can see you're still into him. It's pathetic. Well, he might be nice enough to talk to you, but he's not *into* you. Trust me, *I* know. Once he's officially going out with me, you'll have to stay away from him completely."

"He's not going to ask you out," I said, thinking of the way he'd held my hand moments before and wondering once more what it meant. But I wasn't certain of that statement and Jade pounced on that uncertainty.

"Oh no? Funny that, because we've been spending a

lot of time together rehearsing our screen kiss a *lot*, and not just in rehearsals." Jade gave me a little poke in the shoulder. "Get over him, Ruby. Why would he want a has-been like you? It's me he's into now and don't try and take him because I always get my way – or hadn't you noticed?"

"Oh, I'd noticed," I said, the knowledge bubbling up inside me. "And I know how too."

"What do you mean by that, loser?" Jade asked, narrowing her eyes.

"I mean I know," I said, moving my face a little closer so that this time it was Jade that moved away from me. "I know *everything*."

"Ladies!" Tristan appeared in the doorway, breaking the tension. "Places, please. We've got a lot of work to do and not a lot of time to do it in."

I smiled at Jade and walked back into the rehearsal room. It was a second or two before Jade followed me.

Jade was dreadful for the rest of the rehearsal, forgetting her lines, missing her cues and stumbling in the dance routines. Tristan had to keep on stopping a scene that up until now we had been performing all the way through without any major problems.

"Jade," Tristan said patiently, at the fourth or fifth mistake, "you seem to have lost your focus since the break. Is it something I can help you with? Are you nervous about performing for your father?"

"Don't be so ridiculous!" Jade shrieked, flinging her prop ballet bag on the floor and stamping her feet. "It's not me!" She gestured at the rest of the cast. "I'm not the one who's getting it wrong, it's them, it's *all* of them! Can't you see I'm the only professional here? I want my daddy!"

And with one more stamp of her foot she marched out of the room, leaving the rest of us open-mouthed.

"What did you say to her in the corridor?" Dakshima asked me, wide-eyed, as we watched Tristan bury his head in his hands for a moment. "Whatever it was it really freaked her out."

"Nothing really," I told Dakshima. "I just told her that I *knew*. I didn't say what I knew, just that I did. And judging by the way that she's reacted, *she* must know about the Auto-tune Miracle Microphones, otherwise why would she go mental like that?"

"Unless there's something *else* that she thinks you know, that you don't know, but now she thinks she knows that you know, and knowing *that* is doing her head in," Dakshima whispered.

"Huh?" I looked at Dakshima, who shrugged.

"Meh. I lost track after the second 'know'."

"Right!" Tristan clapped his hands together. "The show must go on and we can't wait for little girls who have tantrums – who's the understudy for Arial?"

Everyone was silent, staring blankly back at Tristan.

"Come on," Tristan said, taping his foot impatiently. "One of the very first things I did was to assign a chorus member to understudy every lead character..." he trailed off and clapped his hand over his mouth.

"I'm totally and completely fired," he said, more to himself than to us. "What with all the rush, I *forgot* to assign understudies! Why didn't any of you tell me? Because you're kids and half of you are amateurs, that's why." Tristan banged his forehead with the heel of his hand. "This is what happens when I get forced into rehearsing a bunch of children for a major show in less than a month. Things get missed, things go wrong. I told Carmen that, but would she listen to me? Does she ever listen to anyone? Of course not – she's Carmen Baptista and she wants to show the whole world that she can do the impossible. Well it won't work, and it's not my fault and I'm still going to get fired!"

"It's probably not that bad," Dakshima piped up, stopping Tristan in mid rant. He paused and looked at her one eyebrow raised. "After all, it's not like Jade's broken her leg or anything. She'll be back. And now you've remembered the understudies you can get them sorted. I bet a load of people here remember all the lines for the main characters, and we all know the songs. Ruby – you know Arial's lines, don't you?" Dakshima dug me in the ribs.

"No, I don't, I can't," I said, as Tristan eyed me. "I don't want to…"

"Want to what?" Tristan asked me hopefully.

"Go on, the guy is having a nervous breakdown and you can help," Dakshima urged me.

"Yes, but I've left show business…"

"Ruby, you are standing in a rehearsal room on the verge of performing live on national TV! Isn't it about time you admitted that the last thing you've done is give up your dream. This is you, it's who you are!" Dakshima told me.

I stood stock still like a rabbit caught in headlights, making Dakshima tut and shake her head. "Tristan!" she called out. "Ruby knows Arial's lines. She knows them all, and the songs and the dance routines too."

"Is that true, Ruby?" Tristan asked.

"Um, yes," I said slowly. "I've been helping Anne-Marie learn her lines and so I've sort of learnt Arial's by accident. I suppose I can step in while Jade calms down if you like, so we can keep going."

"And be my understudy for Jade?" Tristan pushed.

"I suppose so," I said. Dakshima dug me in the ribs again, harder this time "I mean, yes. Yes please, Tristan, I'd love to." And as I said the words, a little thrill rushed through me because I knew I was back. For the first time in weeks, knowing that made me happy.

"Ruby, Ruby, Ruby, you are an *angel*!" Tristan beamed at us all. "Right, let's crack on, Mr Caruso and Miss Baptista are going to be judging us in a matter of hours and we don't want to waste any more time. It's Arial and Sebastian's sweet little kiss scene next..."

I went over and stood next to Danny, and we gazed into each other's eyes.

"I'm so sorry that I let everything that happened to me come between us," I said, speaking Arial's lines. "I never meant for you to think that our friendship wasn't as important to me as the spotlight. Knowing you means everything to me..."

Danny took my hand and said Sebastian's lines. "And I'm sorry that I didn't see how hard everything was for you, that I was stubborn and stupid. You mean so much to me, Ruby..."

"STOP!" Tristan shouted. "Arial, Arial, her name's *Arial* not *Ruby*. Focus, Danny!"

"Um, sorry," Danny said, blushing bright red, which made my cheeks hot too.

"You never have this trouble when you're about to kiss Jade," Tristan said, making everyone giggle. "Take it from the last line *again*, please."

Danny picked up my hand again and took a breath before looking me in the eye again. "And I'm sorry that I didn't see how hard everything was for you, that I was stubborn and stupid. You mean so much to me, Arial – you're my starlight girl."

And as the music of that song began to swell, Danny, that is Sebastian, drew me, I mean Arial, closer to him, bent his head and kissed me softly on the lips.

"Stop!" I dimly heard Tristan say. "STOP!"

Danny and I broke apart. "I got the name right didn't I?" he asked Tristan.

"Yes, but you were so busy kissing Ruby here that you missed the start of the song!"

It took a long time for the whistling, cheering and laughter to stop.

I found it hard to look Danny in the eye since our stage kiss overran, feeling even more confused than ever about how he might or might not feel about me. I was actually glad when Jade came back after about an hour, composed once more.

I saw fury flash across her face when she saw who it who had stepped into her shoes, but she didn't let anyone else see her anger. She apologised first to Tristan and then to the rest of us, telling us that she would never behave like that again. Then she thanked me very politely, even patting me on the back as I went back to my place in the chorus.

I was buzzing. Dakshima was right. Acting, dancing, even singing was really what I wanted to do and it didn't matter how much I tried to pretend I didn't. But right now I was glad to be back in the chorus, because there was very little chance of me having to kiss Danny in front of a whole room of people again while I was there.

Later, as we were having a drink and snack before our performance for Mick and Miss Bapstista, Dakshima, Talitha, Hannah and Adele flocked around me.

"You two were so good together during that scene," Talitha said. "I tell you, either that Danny is a world class actor or he so loves you, Ruby."

"Yeah," Adele said. "And we've all seen *Kensington Heights* – he's not *that* a good an actor." Everyone laughed except me.

"He doesn't like me like that," I said. "Actually I think it's Jade he likes."

"Then why didn't he keep saying Jade's name by mistake," Hannah said.

"It's an easy mistake to make," I said.

"Yeah," Dakshima rolled her eyes. "Rooo-oooby, Airrr-reeee-alll. They sound practically identical." The girls laughed again, and even I smiled.

"The truth is," Hannah said, "you two were much better together than him and her." She yanked a thumb over her shoulder at Jade, who was laughing and chatting with Danny as if nothing out of the ordinary had happened and she hadn't stropped off leaving the rest of us in the lurch. "And that is reason enough for her to hate you even more than normal. You'd better be on the look out, she's bound to be after you."

"Don't worry, I will be," I said, unable to stop thinking about Danny kissing me, I mean Arial.

"Right gang," Tristan called out. "The bus is here. Let's go and show them how hard we've been working."

The cast sat in the rows of seats that had been set up by the production team so we'd have an idea how close the live studio audience would be to us, as we waiting for Mick Caruso and Carmen Baptista to turn up.

As I sat there, I allowed myself to wish it was me leading that cast out on to the stage. More than that, I believed that I could play Arial just as well if not better than Jade. For the first time in a long time I felt confident in myself again – and I knew the microphone *I* had worn while playing Arial was not hooked up to an auto-tune device.

As I sat there in the middle of the TV studio and looked around at its lights and cameras, beautiful and frightening all at the same time, I felt my heart beat faster. I knew that even if all of us left, the studio still wouldn't feel empty. It was as if all the plays and shows filmed there over the last fifty years had left something behind, some sort of imprint, like an energy that vibrated in the air. And as I waited for us to perform I felt as if I was plugged into it and that it was filling me with electricity.

Suddenly one of the lighting engineers switched on a spotlight and for a moment the brightness dazzled me and I had to shield my eyes. Then, as my eyes adjusted, I dropped my hand and tipped my face back, feeling the warmth on my cheeks.

That warmth made me feel as if I might, just might, truly belong there.

Finally Mick Caruso and Carmen Baptista appeared on stage to cheers and applause.

"Well, this is it, we're nearly there," Mick said. "When

I had this idea just over a year ago, almost everybody said I was crazy to create a musical just for under-sixteens. And when I said I wanted to search the nation for the best talent it had, then get the show from the first open audition to casting and then broadcast in three months, they thought I was crazier. But it happened, it *is* happening, and all because you've made it possible. You are all amazing, incredibly talented young people and you've made my impossible dream a reality."

He smiled at us before continuing. "And now you're going to show Carmen and me that the faith that we and the British public have in you is justified. I don't need to tell you how important this premiere is to me. Do your best and don't let me down. Break a leg, people."

As I took my place at the back of the set, I looked at Danny and Jade holding hands centre stage and felt sick inside. Not because Jade said that Danny liked her and was going to ask her out. Perhaps he did, perhaps he didn't. Perhaps it was possible to be kissed by a boy and feel all wonderful and floaty about it inside, while they felt absolutely nothing. But either way, there was nothing I could do to find out what Danny was thinking or feeling until he told me, if he ever did. I felt sick because I knew that whatever happened on this stage in the next 80 minutes, if Jade forgot all of her words and Danny turned out to have two left feet, then they would *still* be leading the show when it was transmitted live in a week's time, whether they deserved it or not. That was what Mick Caruso wanted and he'd use any kind of trickery he could to make it work.

But Jade remembered all of her words and Danny danced like a dream, and as we sung 'Starlight Girl', Jade and Danny's kiss looked pretty convincing to me. And after the big finale of 'Spotlight', the production team, camera operators, costume and make-up people stood on their feet and cheered for us as we took a bow. It should have been an exhilarating and exciting moment and looking around I could see that it was for everybody else.

Only me and Dakshima knew it hadn't been real. Dakshima put her arm around me and whispered. "This show is going to make Jade famous all over the world."

"Do you really think so?" I asked.

"Don't see it going any other way," Dakshima said. "That microphone makes her sound brilliant."

"I know," I said, glancing over at Jade as she hugged Danny hard. "There really is no stopping her now."

We waited and watched as Carmen Baptista and Mick Caruso stood in a huddle on the stage along with Tristan, discussing the run through. Then suddenly Miss Baptista flung her notes in Mick Caruso's face and marched off stage, closely followed by a camera woman from the behind-the-scenes film crew. Mick shrugged and said something to Tristan, who nodded and shrugged.

Finally Mick came to the front of the stage to talk to us.

"Miss Baptista has had to take a break," he said. "She's overcome with emotion and I know how she feels. I want you to know that we could not have been more proud of you if we hand-picked each of you ourselves."

He took a deep breath and for a moment I wondered if he was actually going to cry.

"The first ever live performance world premiere performance of *Spotlight!* will take place in this very studio in a week's time and I want you to know that every single one of you deserves to be in it."

The cast erupted into to cheers and I felt people either side and behind me hugging me and clapping me on the back.

I tuned at looked at Dakshima. "We've got to do something," I said.

"I know," she said. "And I think I've finally worked out what."

Come and step into the...

Spotlight!
The Musical©

Lyrics and music by Mick Caruso

Book by Den Felton

Starring

Danny Harvey   Jade Caruso

Anne-Marie Chance   David Rubenfeld

With

Adele Adebayor, Ruby Parker, Talitha Penny, Hannah Penny,

Dakshima Kour, Gabriel Martinez, Gorkay Mehmet,

Rohan Anderson and Tom Harris

"Because tomorrow belongs to the young!"

Chapter Fourteen

"You are going to do what? I asked Dakshima, open mouthed, as we sat in her bedroom later that night.

"*We* are going to do it. It's a genius plan, isn't it?" she grinned, brushing out her long dark hair.

"But... but you *can't*," I said. "I mean, you literally can't do that – can you?"

"Yeah, I can – it's easy if you have a basic grasp of electronic engineering," Dakshima shrugged.

"You do realise that the show is only two nights away? When, *how* are you going to do this?"

"*We* are going to do it on the night of the show – during the show. That's where the genius part comes in."

I was so astonished by what Dakshima had come up with that I hadn't even thought about whether her plan was even legal, which considering I was once almost arrested for diamond theft, should probably have been one of my first worries.

"It's simple," Dakshima explained. "Each of the Autotune Miracle Microphone's receivers is hooked up to the main sound desk and controlled centrally from there. All we have to do is get to the desk while we are not on set, and while you distract the sound engineer, I'll switch the Auto-tune function off. And hey presto! The studio audience of the world's top celebrities and press, not to mentions millions of viewers around the world, will no longer be listening to angels but to strangled cats. And the truth about Jade and Danny, and Mick Caruso's big scam, will finally be revealed and all wrongs will be righted! So what do you think?"

I didn't say anything for quite a long time, because for quite a long time I didn't know what to say.

"It is a very cunning plan," I began slowly. "And there is an element of genius involved, but... I thought that we'd decided we'd try not to hurt anyone who didn't deserve it. You're talking about wrecking Mick Caruso, Jade and Danny's careers. And the whole musical will be ruined and the all the work that everyone else has put in – you, me, Anne-Marie, Adele – will be for naught."

"For *naught*?" Dakshima raised an eyebrow. "Ruby, you are *such* a lovey. But don't worry because I've thought of that already. It's all in the timing. There are two ensemble numbers before Jade and Danny's first duet so those will go ahead as normal. We will all be great and the audience will love it. Then, during the scene before their first duet, we'll switch off their microphones. It's going to be brutal, but so what if Mick and Jade's reputations are ripped to shreds? They deserve it."

"I'm not sure any thirteen-year-old deserves that," I said, remembering my Hollywood nightmare. "And anyway, what's to stop everyone thinking that the whole cast has been auto-tuned," I said.

"Never gonna happen," Dakshima said. "What's the first thing you showbiz types learn as babies?"

"Get a good agent?"

"That the show must go on, *obviously*." Dakshima looked at me despairingly. "We'll let them mess it up just enough that everyone knows and then we, the rest of the cast and chorus, will pile on stage and save the day. You can sing all of Jade's parts – and relaunch your entire career in one night."

Dakshima seemed so sure of her plan that it was sort of hard to argue what was wrong with it, only something really, really was. It was cruel and unkind, and as much as I disliked Jade, I didn't think I could do anything so horrible to her.

"We can't do it, Dakshima," I said. "Danny doesn't deserve to find out like that. He'd be so hurt and humiliated, his career would be over and he's not even fourteen yet. We can't do that to him or Jade. You're a genius, yes, but you're not an *evil* genius. You know it's not right."

"I knew you'd say that," Dakshima sighed. "In that case there's one other thing we can do."

"What is it?" I asked anxiously.

"Confront them with the truth," Dakshima said. "Give them a chance to drop out of the show."

"You want *me* to tell Danny, my *ex-boyfriend* Danny, who actually I'd quite like to be my current boyfriend again, that he is a fake and that I've known all along?" I asked her in horror.

"It's the only option left. Or let the show go on as planned and do nothing."

"I wish we'd never found out what was going on," I said, miserably.

"Me too," Dakshima said. "But we did and we can't pretend we haven't."

Later that night, while I was supposed to be asleep, I paced up and down the length of my bedroom which, as it wasn't a very long bedroom, wasn't all that helpful. One good thing about Jeremy buying a new house was that I was fairly sure that whenever I stayed over there I'd get a bigger bedroom to pace up and down in.

I just didn't know how to tell Danny. I couldn't think

of a single good way to explain to him that actually he was right about the voice he heard in his head, that it *was* terrible. Oh, and by the way, Mick Caruso was only pretending to love his singing because he had a huge female fan base and because Jade Caruso fancied him.

Danny would be so upset. He'd be *angry*. And I was sure it would be *me* he'd be angry with, because I'd known for a long time and I'd kept it from him. He wouldn't understand that the reason I'd waited so long was because I didn't know *how* to tell him and that being friends with him again was so nice that I didn't want anything, not even the truth, to wreck it.

But when it came to the crunch, what else could I do?

Because of the Auto-tune Miracle Microphone, Nydia hadn't won the number of votes that she needed to beat Jade and was missing out on a chance that she deserved. And millions of people had voted for Jade and Danny because they loved them, because they trusted what they heard and wanted to support them. All of those people had been lied to and betrayed, and that wasn't right either.

Sometimes I got things wrong, said or did the wrong thing. I knew that I could be mean or selfish and unkind, but on the whole I understood right and wrong. Should showbusiness be allowed to cheat and do things the wrong way just because it could? No. It was time for me to be brave, which was going to be tricky because being brave isn't my best thing.

I fished my mobile phone out of my bag and thought for a minute. Scrolling down through the list of names I eventually found the one that I wanted and pressed 'dial'.

After a few rings Nydia answered. "Hi," she said. "Aren't you banned from ringing people after 9 p.m?"

"Yes, but Mum and Jeremy are looking at house details. They won't check on me for ages."

"And I thought you were supposed to be no good at rebelling," Nydia chuckled.

"Anyway what's up?" I ask her. "I haven't seen you much lately."

"I'm OK," Nydia said. "A bit bored. It feels like I'm the only person in all of London who isn't in *Spotlight!*"

"Bummer," I said, feeling worse.

"But it's not all bad news. Because of my performance on the TV I've been asked to audition for the part of a singing alien in *Doctor Who* – how cool is that?"

"Way cool," I said, wondering how to say what I wanted to without sounding weird. "You know, you would make an amazing Arial. And you know that after the TV performance they're thinking of taking the show on tour all over the country? So I was thinking..."

"*What* were you thinking?" Nydia prompted me.

"Well, there might be a part in that for you. Maybe even the part of Arial. You should learn the lines – just in case."

"Maybe," Nydia said. "Then again, maybe I'll be too busy playing a singing alien in *Doctor Who*."

"Just learn the words, OK?" I said pointedly.

"Why?" Nydia was curious. "What do you know, Ruby Parker?"

"Nothing," I lied. "I just feel it in my tummy that you should."

"Sounds like indigestion to me," Nydia said.

Chapter Fifteen

"This is it, choir," Mr Petrelli said, as we finished our lunchtime rehearsal on Friday afternoon. "Your big moment in the sun, or should I say spotlight? Sorry, that's the last time I make that pun, I promise!" We all laughed. "I'm so proud of you. When we started on this journey, you were a bunch of tuneless misfits and now somehow you're the best school choir in the country about to make a TV debut. Don't forget me when you're famous, OK?"

"Actually, sir," Talitha said, glancing around at the rest of us, "we wanted to give you something to say thank you for getting us this far." The boys rustled about and then after a moment produced a carrier bag.

"You were supposed to wrap it!" Hannah said, rolling her eyes.

"You try gift wrapping – it's well hard, man," Gabe said. "We kept ripping the paper."

"Anyway," Dakshima said, taking the bag and handing it to Mr Petrelli. "We hope you like it. "It's a boxed set of Rogers and Hammerstein musicals. Tristan reckons they are the best."

"Only we're not allowed to say so in front of Mr Caruso," Rohan added.

"Guys," Mr Petrelli took the box of DVDs out of the bag and looked at the yellow post-it Gabe had stuck on the packaging. "Cheers for everything from us lot, open brackets, the choir, close brackets."

He smiled at us. "I'm really touched," he said. "And I really, really hope it isn't the end of us working together. Every single one of you has found a voice since you've been here and I'd hate for any one of you to stop singing." He paused and coughed. "And if you're willing, then I'll be here for choir practice every Wednesday lunchtime. Maybe we'll even find another competition to enter, or perhaps put on a musical of our own."

We all looked at each other and nodded.

"Cool," Gabe said.

"A school play would be great," I said, nodding at Mr Petrelli's present. "Maybe we could even try one of those musicals."

"Actually, Ruby," Rohan mumbled. "We got you a thing too."

"Me?" I was surprised.

"Well, we wouldn't have got anywhere if you hadn't

got us all dressed up like idiots and prancing around like nutters," Gabe said. There was another rustle at the back of the room and another carrier bag brought out.

"It's a special pair of legwarmers," Dakshima told me. "Talitha and Hannah knitted them – gold and glittery with sequins, just for you. They're to remind you to never stop doing what you're good at, OK? Because we all know you're brilliant."

I took the glittery legwarmers out of the bag and suddenly my eyes filled up with tears. Maybe it was silly to cry over a pair of legwarmers, maybe I was just being a lovey again and exactly the sort of drama queen that Danny always said I was, but to know that these people believed in me made me the happiest I had been for a long time.

"Blimey, don't blub," Gabe said, putting an arm round me.

"Thanks everyone," I said, sniffing loudly. "Thanks for letting me be part of your choir and your school."

"We'll miss you when you go back the Academy," Dakshima said.

"Go back the Academy?" I echoed. "I'm not doing that – what ever gave you that idea?"

"So get I'll my full choir back after Easter?" Mr Petrelli asked me.

"Of course you will, sir," I said. "We're team aren't we?"

"Have you got the cheque for the twenty-thousand pounds yet, sir?" Dakshima asked him casually as we walked out of school.

"I think so," Mr Petrelli said. "All that sort of business goes through the head."

"Have you cashed it yet?" Dakshima persisted.

"Why?"

"No reason." Dakshima smiled brightly at Mr Petrelli before mumbling to me, "That Mick Caruso might want it back otherwise."

"Well, Mrs Petrelli and I have our tickets, we are really looking forward to seeing you tomorrow," Mr Petrelli called out as he climbed into his car. "Good luck – break a leg!"

"*So?*" Dakshima asked me.

"So?" I said heavily, full of dread about what I had to do.

"Are you going round there now?" she said. We'd agreed the night before that I should tell Danny first, and then the two of us would go and confront Jade and her dad.

"Going where?" Talitha and Hannah appeared at our shoulders.

"Oh, nowhere—" I began.

"She's going round to see Danny," Dakshima told them.

"Oooh, are you going to tell him you *lurve* him," Talitha teased.

"No!" I said. "I'm just going to ask him something about the show."

"To practise the kissing scene with you in case Jade breaks her mouth?" Hannah giggled, making Dakshima laugh.

"I am just going to talk to him, that's all," I said, stoutly walking way from the group. "Now good day to you all."

"Good day!" the girls shrieked with laughter.

"You lovey types are all the same," Dakshima called after me as I trudged down the street. "Good luck, Rubes!"

"Thanks," I said under my breath. "I'm going to need it."

"Ruby," Danny said. "Wow, I was just going to call you."

"Were you?" I asked nervously.

"I thought you might want to meet me in the café for a hot chocolate." Danny said. "You know, just to talk and hang out."

"Good," I said, with a shy smile. "Because I'm not sure you're allowed to do much else in a café."

Danny laughed. "So," he said smiling at me. "You're here again."

"Yes I am," I said. I was getting a distinct feeling of *dejá vu*, sure that Danny and I had had almost this exact exchange the last time I tried to tell him about the Autotune Miracle Microphone. That last conversation hadn't worked out so well; we had fallen out without even even making up to begin with, and I *still* hadn't managed to tell him.

What ever happened now, I knew that this time I had to tell him, however it ended. If I failed, Danny Harvey, a boy that I still really cared about, would find out the truth for himself on Saturday night in front of an audience of thousands.

"Danny," I said, steeling myself, "I've come to tell you something important."

"Really?" Danny's smile grew uncertain, probably because I sounded so serious. "OK," he said slowly. "But would you mind if I told you something important first? Because if you hear what I've got to say, it might change what you've got to say."

"I don't think it will…" I said uncomfortably.

"Please, Ruby," Danny said. I shrugged and nodded. "It's just that I wanted to say sorry for dumping you for Melody. I was an idiot… again."

"Pardon?" I blinked at him, realising ten seconds too late that he was trying to apologise for breaking up with me.

"Yes," Danny took a step closer. "When you went away I felt jealous and left out and all that stuff with Sean was more of an excuse from me to be angry with you than a proper reason. I suppose I did get a bit big-headed about the number one and *Kensington Heights* and all that. And I suppose I thought you didn't care about me any more. Pretty immature right?"

I paused to take in what he had just said. "Well, yes, actually," I had to agree.

"The thing is," Danny went on. "I really miss hanging out with you, and maybe you came round here to tell me that you don't want to hang out with me, or that you don't like me. But whatever you say, I wanted to tell you that I do still like you. A lot." Danny shrugged. "Your turn."

I looked at Danny's dark eyes sparkling at me and said the truth out loud.

"Danny... you can't actually sing." The words tumbled out of my mouth. "The only reason you're the lead in the show is because Jade wants you there. She got her dad to give you the part so that she could get her claws into you. When you sing it's not your real voice that you are hearing come out of the speakers. It's fed through a thing called an Auto-tune Miracle Microphone that adjusts your voice instantly and makes you sound really good."

I paused to take a breath and glanced at the expression on Danny's face. It was very quiet and still.

"When you recorded your hit single, you know they tweaked your voice in the recording studio – you told me. And you know when before you said that in your head you always sound terrible when you sing?" I went on, unable to stop talking, like my voice was a runaway train careering downhill towards disaster. "Well, that's because you *do* sound terrible. Look, you're an amazing boy and a great actor and even an OK dancer, but you really *can't* sing. And neither can Jade. And me and Dakshima just thought we should tell everyone what we know – starting with you…"

Finally I came juddering to a halt and braced myself.

Danny laughed uneasily. "Look, that's not funny." he said.

"I know," I said miserably. "But it's true. Dakshima and I found out during the auditions. We sneaked upstairs to try and peek at the judges and you were one of the people we saw. We *heard* you sing without a microphone and you weren't good, Danny. But Mick Caruso told you that you were and that you were going through the live final. We heard him tell Elaine Emmerson that he was putting you through not because you could sing but because Jade wanted you to play the part of Sebastian opposite her Arial. I'm not trying to hurt you, Danny, because that's totally the last thing I want to do, but Dakshima and I can't keep it to ourselves any more. Jade doesn't deserve that part. She and her dad have cheated to make sure she gets everything she wants, including you as her leading man."

"You're crazy!" Danny flared up. "I'm not stupid. I know that you can change the way a voice sounds in a recording studio, but you can't do that day after day at rehearsals. Or on the live final. I was singing *live*, Ruby."

"Into an Auto-tune Miracle Microphone," I said. "Haven't you noticed that you and Jade always have a different style of microphone? And that you are the *only* ones who do? That's what makes you sound so good."

"You are lying." Danny shook his head and I could see fury boiling in his dark eyes. "You've been in rehearsal with us for weeks, Ruby. We've all heard the same thing."

"Because you were always wearing the microphone…" I thought for a moment. "Come with me and I'll prove it."

"What? Go where with you?" Danny asked me.

"To the rehearsal studio." I explained, looking at my watch and wondering how long it would be before Mum noticed I was late. "Where I can show you the truth."

* * *

It took some persuading to get Eileen, the security lady, to let us in unsupervised, but once I explained to her that I'd left my mum's birthday present in the studio and that her birthday was today, she let us in. I had fifteen minutes and no more because children weren't allowed unaccompanied in the building and she'd get fired if anyone found out.

"You are getting very good at lying in your old age," Danny said, as he followed me towards our rehearsal room. The building wasn't empty, there were other rehearsals for other shows, both TV and theatre, going on all over the building. Our mission was to try and avoid being spotted by any of them.

"I don't *want* to have to lie or come out here, when I know Mum is going to kill me for being late and not telling her where I've gone. She'll probably think I've caught a flight to Acapulco or somewhere," I told him in a low voice as we crept along the corridors. "And then I'll get the talk about whether I'm happy and if I'm planning another stupid trip, so I am *never* late, because I never want Mum to worry that much about me again. Except for now, because I have to make you see the truth. *That's* how serious this is."

We entered the room and I switched on a couple of

lights. Once I could see well enough, I turned on both sets of microphone receivers, hooking them up to the speakers like I had seen the engineer do a hundred times.

Using some of the special tape that was used to fix the microphones to just below our hairlines, I fixed both types on to Danny, who submitted despite his anger. Standing close, we looked at each other for a second in the half light and I couldn't help thinking that the moment could have been so different. But it was too late to turn back now.

"This is ridiculous," he said.

"Is it?" I asked him, going to the control panel. "Then why are you here? You must know that something isn't quite right or you wouldn't have come with me." I turned up one of the microphones.

"This is the Auto-tune Miracle Microphone," I told him. "Go on, sing."

His eyes flashing, Danny let rip a few lines from, 'Love Gets it Wrong Every Time.'

I got the distinct impression that he was trying to tell me something, but I couldn't worry about that now. I had to stay focused.

"That sounded really good," I told him. "Now I'm turning the Auto-tune off, and the regular microphone on. Try again."

Danny only managed to sing a few words before

stuttering to a stop. "It's broken," he said, ripping the mic off.

"It's not, Danny." I picked it up and sang a few bars into it. My voice sounded exactly like it always did.

Danny bent his head and crossed his arms across his chest for a moment, before looking up at me. "They've lied to me," he said quietly. "Made a right fool of me and manipulated me."

"Yes," I said reluctantly.

"And you've known for weeks, Ruby," he continued accusingly. "You've known all this time and you didn't tell me. I bet you thought it was hilarious that I was making such a fool of myself."

"Danny please – it's not like that!" I protested. "I *did* try and tell you, but you got the wrong end of the stick and then we started to be friends again I didn't want us falling out again."

"So why are you telling me now?" Danny asked me. "Why couldn't you wait until the show was finished."

"Because you and Jade have got parts in a show that you don't really deserve and people like Nydia are missing out. Besides, if I didn't tell you Dakshima was planning to turn off your microphones during your first duet, and then the whole world would have found out the truth in the worst possible way. And I couldn't let that happen to you, or Jade – even if you both hate me for it."

"You're both crazy!" Danny exclaimed angrily.

"We're not. We're just trying to do the right thing. Can't you see that?"

"No, but I am tone deaf apparently," Danny said bitterly. "Look, you can't tell anyone else about this."

"Why not?" I asked him. "Do you still want to go ahead and play Sebastian, even now you know?"

"No, I'm not a hypocrite and I won't be pushed around like that by anyone," Danny said. "But Jade has worked so hard on the show and, I swear to you, she doesn't know about those microphones either."

I laughed out loud. "Of course she does! Look, Danny, I know that Jade has been acting all sweetness and light with you, but that's all it is – an act. All that rubbish she came out with about auditioning like everyone else, about not wanting any special favours? Her dad *made* this musical for her; he gave her the lead *and* the leading man she wanted. You. Of course she knows. It was probably her idea."

"That's rubbish." Danny was adamant. "I've spent a lot of time with her recently and she's not like you think. You… you're jealous!"

"Jealous!" I gasped. "How did you work that one out!"

"Because you're about to wreck a show that a ton of people have put a load of effort into, just to be spiteful!"

"I'm *not* jealous! I just think that the lead parts should go to the right people."

"Like you, you mean," Danny said looking at me so harshly that for a moment I couldn't speak.

"No, Danny," I said. "Like Nydia and that other boy for the live final – Callum Thingummy. I just want to do what's right. And I'm going round to Jade's house to talk to her now. If you don't want to come with me, that's up to you."

"Oh, I'm coming," Danny said. "If Jade has to know then we'll tell her together. And I promise, she'll be just as angry as me."

"Fine!" I spat, angry that Danny was being so protective of Jade. "OK, we'll go and tell, and then she can explain to you how she's known all along about everything."

"Fine!"

"Good!"

As we turned off the equipment and I flicked off the lights, my phone rang. I took it out of my pocket and my heart sank further.

"Hi, Mum," I said, trying to sound a lot brighter than I felt. "Am I late?"

"You are an *hour* late," Mum replied, her voice a mixture of worry and anger. "Home by 5.30 after school we agreed.

When you said you were popping round to Danny's, you didn't say you'd be late. Where *are* you exactly?"

I bit my lip. I didn't want to admit that Danny and I had got the bus to other side of London where we were currently wandering around a rehearsal studio without adult supervision.

"Danny and I are sorting a few things out for tomorrow and we're just going to see Jade, and then I'll be back."

"Jade Caruso? You don't even like her, do you?"

"I know, but I have to go, Mum," I said. "It's really important. It's about the show tomorrow."

"In that case you won't mind me coming to meet you there," Mum said. "I'll pick you up and bring you home."

"Mum I don't need you to—"

"No arguments, Ruby, That's what's going to happen," Mum told me. "See you then."

"Right." I looked at Danny. "Let's get this over with."

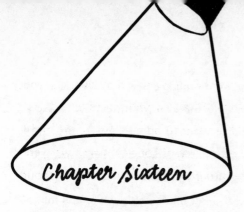

Chapter Sixteen

Anne-Marie's house is big and grand, but compared to Mick Caruso's rock star palace it was practically a bungalow. This place was so big that it didn't have gardens, it had grounds, complete with a half-mile driveway leading to the grand front door.

Because we didn't have much time before my mum turned up, Danny and I got a taxi to Jade's. But it turned out that we only had enough money to pay the cab driver to take us down about a third of the drive, so we had to jog the rest.

"I can't believe you've done this to me, Ruby," Danny puffed bitterly as we approached. "You of all people!"

"I'm not the one who did it," I defended myself as Danny rang the bell. "It's Jade and her dad."

"Whatever. You knew and you didn't tell me," Danny said.

Before I could reply, Jade answered the door, which surprised me because I was expecting some snooty butler.

"Hi, I saw it was you on the security TV," she beamed at Danny, before eyeing me distastefully. "What's *she* doing here?"

"She's told me something pretty radical," Danny said. "And now she needs to tell you too."

"Something radical, hey?" Jade said, waving us into a grand hallway, complete with a huge chandelier dangling above our heads. "Is it that she's woken up and discovered a dress sense?"

"Jade," Danny chided. "You don't have to act like that around me, or Ruby, OK?"

Jade's hard face softened as she looked at Danny and I realised for the first time that she really *did* like him. I could see by the look on her face that he was more than just a prize to be won. That didn't exactly make me warm to her.

"Come through to the den," Jade said, ignoring me and smiling at Danny. "Dad's around somewhere, but he never usually bothers me when I'm in there."

She led us down some steps to a big pink-painted room containing a huge TV screen, games consoles and several computers. There was thick cream carpet on the floor with big, fat bean bags scattered around.

"So, what's this radical news then?" Jade asked me, sinking gracefully into one that was cerise-coloured.

"Jade, remember that day I told you that I knew your

secret, when you freaked and walked out of rehearsal?"

Jade looked uncomfortable. "No," she said.

"Yes, you do. Anyway, I've told Danny. Now he knows too."

Jade visibly crumpled. "How did you find out?" she asked miserably. Her expression was so different from the one I had expected that for a moment I wondered if I was really talking to Jade's secret twin, like had once happened to my character in *Kensington Heights*.

"You *know*?" Danny asked her, shocked.

"Of course I know," Jade said, looking at him unhappily. "I just don't know how *she* knows how terrified I am of walking out on that set in front of millions of people and singing. I'm all right in rehearsal, but to actually *do* it? I just don't know if I'm ready, Danny. Something doesn't feel quite right, but how can I explain that to Dad? How can I let everyone else down because of my nerves? I don't know how I'm going to get through on the night."

Danny and I looked at each other, confused.

"I thought I'd hidden my fear really well," Jade said miserably. "But Ruby guessed, and now you know and you're afraid that I'm going to mess it up and wreck the show. Well, I'm afraid of that too."

"What are you on about?" I asked her.

"I'm so scared," Jade told Danny. "I know that I came through the auditions like everyone else and that I've earned my place, but it didn't feel real – even with the public vote. And my dad's so famous and so good at what he does. It's a lot to live up to."

"You are good," I said, slow-clapping Jade's lost little girl speech.

"What do you mean?" she asked me, flicking me a worried glance.

"You are the most amazing actress," I told her. "And Jade, there is nothing to be 'scared' about, because with those acting skills it doesn't matter that you can't sing for toffee. You really don't need to cheat to get parts."

"What?" Jade asked. "Why are you saying that?"

"I told you she doesn't know, Ruby," Danny said. "Leave her alone."

"She does know," I said.

"Know what?" Jade demanded, getting up and stamping her foot in the old Jade style. I sighed and spelled out everything that I'd just told Danny, and I watched as her face drained of colour and her eyes grew wide with horror.

Then I realised. Jade was not *that* good an actress. Danny was right, she hadn't known about the Auto-tune Miracle Microphone either.

"It can't be true," Jade said. "Daddy got me special singing lessons back when the musical was in preproduction. He got me a new teacher who could bring out my true voice."

I looked at Danny and shook my head. "The truth is that your signing voice is just as average as it always was, and that the only reason you sound OK is because your dad fitted you up with an Auto-tune Miracle Microphone."

"I've heard of those," Jade said. "Some pop bands who can't sing well live use them."

"And some musical stars whose daddy gave them a musical to star in use them too, Jade."

Jade shook her head. "I told you, I've been having lessons. He's a brilliant teacher – he's taught me how to sing for a musical, how to use a..." Jade trailed off. "A microphone. At every single lesson I always sang into a microphone."

She looked at me and Danny, then went to the den door and swung it open so hard it banged against the wall.

"DADDY!" she shrieked up the stairs. "GET DOWN HERE NOW!"

* * *

"Please tell me she's lying," Jade stormed at her father after confronting him with what I'd told her. "Please tell me that this jumped-up, jealous, frumpy little cow is making all of this up and everything she says is wrong."

Mick Caruso looked at me and rubbed his chin with his hand. "How did you find out?" he asked me, causing Jade to clap her hands over her mouth.

"Me and another girl overheard Danny's audition," I explained. "And afterwards you told Elaine Emmerson that you were going to put him through because Jade told you to."

"No, I said I was going to do it because that's what my little girl wanted," Mick said. "She told me it would be her dream come true, but she never asked me to do anything. I just wanted to make her happy."

"So happy you'd fix results, fake votes and lie to the public?" I asked.

Mick Caruso thought for a moment. "Look, I've created a musical that's going to give a lot of kids a lot of fun. Why shouldn't I give my own child that chance too? So I pulled a few strings here and there, altered a few of the facts to make it happen. But I never rigged the phone vote. More people voted for Jade and Anne-Marie than Nydia, even it was only a handful. At the end of the day – that's showbusiness, right, Ruby? Sometime it's about who you know."

"But I *told* you I didn't want any special help," Jade protested. "I told you I wanted to audition like everyone else. I wanted to make you proud of me."

"I know, love," Mick Caruso said. "And your acting and dancing are as good as everyone else's. You just need a little bit of extra help with your voice, like Danny here. And what does it really matter, if the audience is getting a good show?"

"It matters because it's a lie!" Jade said tearfully. "It matters because for the first time in my life I thought that I could do something as well as you. And now I find out that the whole thing is made up! How could you do that to me, Dad? How *could* you?"

I watched as Jade ran into Danny's arms and he hugged her tightly.

"I'm sorry, Jade," Mick Caruso said. "I thought it would make you happy. I promise that every other single kid in that show deserves to be there."

"And a few who aren't in it, deserve to be there too," I said, watching miserably as Danny stood with arms around Jade.

"The question is," Mick Caruso said turning to me, "what do you want to do about it? Can't we all just carry on? The show's tomorrow."

"I can't," Danny said immediately, dropping his

arms from around Jade. "I've really, really enjoyed the rehearsing and the experience has meant a lot to me. But I'm not going on TV and pretending like this. I won't tell anyone as long as you put things right. As for me – I'm resigning."

Mick looked at his teary daughter and held out his arms to her. Jade ran to him, flinging her arms around his middle and sobbing even louder

"I don't want to do it either," Jade said. "I was already too nervous when I thought I *could* sing. There's no way I can go on in front of millions knowing it's only a piece of equipment standing between me and complete failure. I'm sorry, Daddy, I don't want to let you down."

"It's me who's let you down," Mick said, hugging her. "I never thought it would get this out of hand!" He turned to me. "Look, Ruby, if the press find out about the microphones, then the show will never air and all of those kids who have worked so hard will be out of a job. It's a good show, you know it is. So how about you forget what you know and let the show go on without Danny or Jade?"

"I don't know what to do," I said unhappily.

"Perhaps I can help make up your mind," Mick Caruso said. "Like I said, sometimes showbiz is about who you know and not what you can do. How about we make a deal. You and your friend forget everything you know, and you can take Jade's place as Arial in the premiere of *Spotlight!* tomorrow. You'll be Ruby Parker Musical Star – what do you say?"

Chapter Seventeen

The lights went down and I held my breath as I listened to the chatter of the audience settle into silence. I felt my stomach knot and twist.

This was it, this was the moment that we had all been working intensely towards. We were about to broadcast live to millions of viewers all around the world. And even if it hadn't quite turned out as I expected, I was desperate, absolutely *desperate*, for the audience to love the show as much as I did.

I felt adrenaline surge through my body as the lights came up and the spotlight picked out the show's new leading lady.

Nydia stood there as if she was born for the part of Arial, not just intensely rehearsed for just one day like she actually had.

I'd considered Mick Caruso's offer of the lead in exchange for my silence for about two seconds. I didn't want to wreck the show for everybody else who had worked so hard on it, but more than that I knew I didn't want to take a part I hadn't won fairly or squarely.

"You have to make everything fair," I'd told Jade's dad. "You have ask Nydia to take the part of Arial, because she would have won the phone vote if Jade hadn't cheated."

"There's no way she'll be ready," Mick Caruso had protested. "It will be a disaster."

"No, it won't," I told him. "Nydia's been learning the lines and she can pick up direction faster than anyone I know. And you have to offer Danny's role to Callum."

"Callum's not available – he's got a part in Joseph," Mick said.

"Well, Gabe Martinez is Danny's understudy, and he's been doing an amazing job. He's been really great as Sebastian."

"I've noticed him," Mick said. "Do you think he's up to it?"

I nodded. "He'll be brilliant." I'd said it, but I was unable to look at Danny.

"Agreed," Mick said.

"And from now on you have to give Jade credit for what she is good at and understand that she doesn't need you to buy her success for her. She's got the talent and the guts to make it happen herself."

"I have?" Jade had looked at me suspiciously.

"Yes," I said grudgingly. "Look, Jade, you and I don't

get on, but you have got talent. Just not for singing.

"Ruby's right," Mick said.

"I know," I said. "And if you do all of those things I'm fairly sure that Dakshima and I will be OK about everything and never mention it again." I said.

"And what about you?" Mick Caruso asked me. "What do you want?"

I smiled at him.

"I want to be in the chorus with my school choir," I said. "Because this time, that's where I belong. *Next* time I'll be going for the lead."

"She's great, isn't she?" Anne-Marie whispered in my ear as we watched Nydia and Gabe singing from off set "It's all going so well isn't it?"

"Really, really well," I said. "And you are brilliant as Serena too."

"I know!" Anne-Marie bounced a little. "I still can't believe Jade had to drop out at the last minute. And that Nydia got called for her part! It's perfect – the three of us working together at last!"

"Well, you know there were only a few votes between Nydia and Jade, apparently," I said. "It's a shame Jade got laryngitis, but Nydia's brilliant."

"I'm so excited," Anne-Marie said. "We're bound to get discovered now! I'll need your help – you know, with the fame, the press, the pressure and all that lark."

"Of course I'll help," I said. "I've always wanted a famous friend. *Another* one, I mean."

We were silent as we watched Nydia finish her solo and the audience burst into applause.

"I feel really sorry for Danny having to pull out from the show with that knee injury," Anne-Marie said, "but on the other hand, I can't imagine Nydia having to kiss him, even just acting. Bleugh!"

"Oh, I don't know," I whispered, glancing at the front row of the studio audience where Jade and Danny were sitting together. "I can think of worse things."

My mum had been there to pick me up at Jade's house exactly when she said she would and she offered Danny a lift home too, which he'd accepted.

As we had pulled up outside Danny's house I got out of the car to say goodbye without Mum listening.

"Danny, do you really hate me?" I asked.

Danny looked at me with those dark intense eyes that made my heart flutter.

"Don't ask me that now," he said. "I know I'm angry and that's about all I know."

"I'm so sorry I didn't tell you before. And, Danny, I…"

I trailed off, not knowing how to finish that sentence.

"Well, I'll see you at the show, I guess," Danny said. "Goodbye." He didn't look at back at me once as he walked into the house.

"Is Danny still upsetting you?" Mum asked me as we drove home.

"I think this time I upset him," I told her, staring out of the window.

"Don't worry love," Mum said. "It'll all come out in the wash.

But this time I was fairly sure I'd blown things with Danny for good and I'd have to get used to knowing that all over again.

At the end of the show the whole cast took a bow as the studio audience yelled and cheered shouting, "Encore!" and "Bravo!" Nydia and Anne-Marie beamed as Mick presented them each with bouquet of pink roses.

"Well, I'm glad I didn't have to do all that wire swapping and turning stuff on and off business," Dakshima said as we got ready to go to the after-show party being held in a hotel over the road. "It was much more fun being in the show than wrecking it. Besides I think it's all worked out for the best, don't you?"

I looked at Danny, who was just ahead of us, his arm linked with Jade's.

"Mostly," I said. "Mostly it has."

The party was full of famous people. Jeremy was there of course, with Mum, but also all the old *Kensington Heights* faces, a bunch of ex-*Hollyoaks* actors and reality show has-beens, and there were rumours of some big announcement by Mick Caruso.

I couldn't wait to tell Anne-Marie and Nydia how great they'd been, but they were both surrounded by admirers. As I walked past one TV crew we heard the reporter say, "Tonight a star was born…"

I wondered who they were talking about.

It had been such a wonderful, exciting evening, but suddenly I felt overwhelmed by everything. I needed a little bit of time to myself, to think. I edged out of the crowded room and, walking down the corridor, found a door marked Private. Once upon a time I would have never dreamed of opening it, but since my escape from Hollywood I realised that I'd become a lot better at rebelling.

I tried the handle and opened it, finding an empty office. I was sure no one would mind if I sat there for a moment, drinking my cranberry juice and collecting my thoughts.

When I had started at Highgate Comprehensive I'd been totally sure that I wanted to give up acting and showbusiness for good. Hollywood had left me feeling battered and bruised. After everything that had happened there I didn't think I had the strength, let alone the talent, to keep trying.

But I was wrong. Because it was in the theatre or on a TV or film set where I really belonged and felt like myself. Acting, performing, was in my blood and in every heartbeat, and although I knew that the road ahead would be tough and that I wouldn't always succeed, I also knew I couldn't give it up.

I had to keep on trying, because the one thing I *couldn't* give up was being me.

Suddenly I wanted to find Mum and tell her that.

As I stepped back out into the corridor I came face to face with Danny, looking all James Bondish again, so handsome in a dinner suit and tie. He stopped when he saw me, then walked a couple of steps closer.

"There you are," he said. "I've been looking for you."

"Really?" I said, wishing I didn't sound quite so surprised by the news.

"I was pretty horrible to you," Danny said. "And I didn't mean it. I was... in shock."

"I know," I said. "I don't think I treated you very well

either. I should have told you straight way instead of waiting for…"

"Waiting for what, Ruby?" Danny asked me.

"Waiting for you to ask me out again, I suppose," I said, blushing.

"And if I had asked you out, would you have said yes?" Danny asked.

"I—"

"Don't answer that," Danny said. "I'm being a coward and I mustn't be. Answer this instead." He smiled and me and took a breath. "Ruby Parker, would you like to go out with me?"

"RUBY PARKER!"

Before I could reply, I heard someone yell my name from behind. I turned around and found Mick Caruso approaching, followed by a beaming Nydia and Anne-Marie.

"You'll never believe this," Anne-Marie squealed.

"Believe what?" I asked.

"I just got a call from a big studio in the USA," Mick told me. "They saw the live broadcast – and they want to make a movie of Spotlight! in Hollywood."

"That's fantastic!" I said. "That's so exciting."

"That's not all," Mick said. "They were so impressed with the cast of tonight's show that they want all the leads to audition for parts. It's not a done deal, there'll be screen tests and plenty of American competition – but they're going to fly you all out there."

My jaw dropped and I hugged Anne-Marie and Nydia hard. "You two are so amazing!" I said squeezing. "I *know* you'll take America by storm."

"You can't have heard me properly," Mick said. "The studios want *you* to try out too. For the part of Arial."

"*Me?*" I was bemused. "Why me? I was only in the chorus."

"A producer who'd seen that film, *The Lost Treasure of King Arthur*, spotted you in the chorus. Hasn't anyone told you what a cult hit that film is with teens all across the USA? They want you back in Hollywood, Ruby. They want to give you another chance. And we're not just talking film opportunities here, girls. We're talking single releases, a live tour – the works."

"Go back to Hollywood?" I said. "To compete against Nydia and Anne-Marie and goodness knows who else for a part? I don't know if I can. I don't know if I *want* to."

"Well, it's up to you," Mick said. "But I seem to remember you saying that the next time there was a lead part on offer, you'd be going for it."

"Imagine, Ruby, all of us going to Hollywood together! How wild is *that*?" Nydia laughed.

"But what we don't all get parts, what then?" I said.

"Well, it wouldn't be the first time," Anne-Marie said. "Look, friends like us don't let a little competition come between us, do we? Come *on*, Ruby – it wouldn't be the same with out you."

"I'll have to think about it," I said.

"You do that," Mick said. "But for now I have to get my stars back to the party. The whole world is waiting to meet them."

I turned to round to talk to Danny, but he wasn't there. I had no idea if he still wanted me to answer his question and besides, I was still reeling from Mick Caruso's unbelievable news.

I took a deep breath.

Could I do it? Could I really go back to Hollywood and try again?

The truth was I didn't know.

Turn the page to sing along with *Spotlight! The Musical*

SPOTLIGHT

ALONE IN A CROWD

LOVE GETS IT WRONG EVERY TIME

Many thanks to Tom and Polly Harris for their musical inspiration and all their hard work.

Catch up with all of Ruby's
celebrity adventures!

Ruby Parker

Soap Star

Everyone thinks I have the Perfect Life.
I'm Ruby Parker, Soap Star.
But real life isn't like television...

www.harpercollinschildrensbooks.co.uk

Catch up with all of Ruby's
celebrity adventures!

Ruby Parker

Film Star

I used to be Ruby Parker, Soap Star.
Now I'm trying to be Ruby Parker, Movie Star.
But what if I turn out to be Ruby Parker,
No Use At All?

Catch up with all of Ruby's
celebrity adventures!

Ruby Parker

Hollywood
Star

Hollywood is just like you read about.
It's big and shiny and fast – and, to be honest,
a bit scary. Now I know why they say it
changes people. I think it's changing me...

www.harpercollinschildrensbooks.co.uk